Long Walk Off a Short Pier

STEPHANIE M. HOLLAND

DEDICATION

This book is dedicated to the memory of my real "Grams", Kathleen Duncan. Without her, I would not have had the strength or encouragement to pursue my dreams and fight for what I believe in.

ACKNOWLEDGMENTS

First and foremost, I must give thanks to God, and his son, Jesus Christ, for bestowing the writing desire, talent, and ability within me. I also give thanks to my ancestors who passed on the genetics of wisdom, strength, and endurance to persevere. I wish to acknowledge the real life inspiration behind the character "Javier". Without all that I went through with him, I would not have had the motivation to have written such an engaging story of discovery of self. Next, great thanks go out to Antonette Poole Bruno, Myra Watson, Tanya Johnston, Thomasine Owens, and Nicholette "Nikki" (Newman) Hammond. You guys have inspired me in ways I can't put into words. Thanks for being there, and sometimes not being there (HA HA). I would also like to thank Mr. Lew Berry for all of his encouragement to continue writing and not throw this book away after all of the time and effort spent on trying to get it into print. At this time I would like to also thank all of the hateful teachers that I had over the years who were anything but encouraging. It is also their lack of faith that propelled my ambition to write even more. To all of the other individuals out there who doubted me, my ability to succeed, or just did not believe in me – I ask, "HOW YA LIKE ME NOW?"

WAKE UP!

I parked my car at the end of the driveway and proceeded to walk up the walkway to Javier's door. I had my keys in my hand and as always, the iron security gate was unlocked. I opened it and put my key in the bottom lock and turned the knob. I entered the foyer and saw his daughters, Serena and Lish, home from school, as expected. Serena spoke to me and I proceeded up the steps to the bedroom, looking for Javier. Usually he would have been home from work by now, but I dismissed my crazy thoughts by rationalizing that he probably just stopped by the cleaners or something on his way home. I took off my shoes and slid them under the king size bed. I heard a faint sound in the distance, like a big semi-truck backing up, "beep, beep, beep." I went back down the steps and peeked out the living room window. There was a big moving truck backing into the driveway just past my car, heading straight for the garage door. I dashed back upstairs and slipped back on the first shoes I could grab and ran back outside into the driveway. Before I could get to the back of the moving truck, a frenzied woman came stomping around from the passenger's side. The driver got out and opened the back of the trailer. She came up to the edge of the walkway with her mahogany brown skin, puffy hair, and take charge attitude, "Who the hell are you?" I looked behind me and to the left and the right, because I just knew this heifer wasn't talking to me! I said, "Excuse me?" She said, "I

1

didn't stutter. Who the hell are you and what are you doing at my house?" I looked at her, astonished, "Your house? What do you mean; your house? This is Javier's house, thank you, and last time I checked I was welcomed here, I can't say the same about you." Next thing I knew, this heifer looked like she was going to charge into me. I quickly took my ready stance and put up my guard. Hey, 20 years of karate, 3rd degree black belt, and I was going to let some "Sapphire" come along and take full advantage of me? OH HELL NO! When she saw I was a force to reckon with she stopped in her tracks. I may be a little petite 5' 3" inches tall, 125 pounds to her 5' 10" Amazon - Lane Bryant stature, but I can hold my own if pushed in a corner. When she retreated, I headed back in the house and grabbed my cell phone and called Javier. He didn't answer, that was suspicious. By this time, the Amazon woman was standing in the driveway, evidently also calling Javier, who I began to suspect, was enjoying the prospect of the two of us clashing and then coming home to the aftermath of a violent duel to the death over him. Unfortunately, the satisfaction would not be his. I put the cell phone in my pocket and headed back outside toward the Amazon woman. She had the nerve to tell me, "I don't know what Javier has told you but we are very much together. We're about to build a house together when he sells this one." Just before I could say anything, Javier pulled up at the edge of the driveway, right behind my car.

Then I woke up…

The following night I fell asleep after much effort and endless tossing and turning. Javier was away training US Marshals at the academy. I had another nightmare. I was climbing up a ladder to his back window, a big picture window to his bedroom. I looked in and saw another woman sleeping alongside him, sleeping like she belonged there. Then I woke up. Someone was clearly trying to send me a warning. It's unfortunate that I was too hard headed to listen and take action early in the game. In the weeks that followed, I discovered that the woman in the dream, who I originally assumed to be his ex-wife that he had his daughters with, was a new woman. This new woman and Javier had been planning to build a life together. I had been having a gnawing feeling in the pit of my stomach that Javier was less than

100% committed. I just never felt the true incentive to act on researching. I started having a series of dreams about him with other women. I thought it was my overactive imagination and that I was just in denial. I didn't want to believe that a man who seemingly showed this much interest, had this much going for him, and was such a people person, would slip out of my grasp. Maybe I should not have tried to hold on so tight.

PROGRESSION

All of the signs were there. I mean, in the beginning, Javier and I had a wonderful relationship. He seemed really into me. We used to go out on the town. When his buddy from his academy days got married, he took me with him and introduced me to everyone as his fiancé. He would call me just to hear my voice. There was never a weekend that we didn't spend some kind of time together. I had known Javier for a while before we ever crossed the line from friends to lovers. I didn't realize that our meeting at the job wasn't the first time we ever saw each other. We had actually both been at the same wedding, years before. I made sure he was fully divorced before I got involved. I was really skeptical about him, because I know what happens when friends turn to lovers and then it doesn't work out. You can't just go back to being friends like everything is ok, yet I threw caution to the wind and went full steam ahead. Big mistake! However, Javier was what I needed at the time, after my relationship with Erick went down in flames and my divorce was final. I had been a lonely single mother for a few years and I was ready to be loved again. Javier was no stranger to me. We had been casual friends when I first took the job at DOJ, but I couldn't bring myself to let him into my world until circa 2003. It was a scary time for me. Javier capitalized on my vulnerability. He had been pursuing me, off and on, since I stepped on the job in 1995. Nothing else was going on in my life, so eventually I just gave in.

I guess I had a false sense of security. Javier was handsome by all measures. Even my religious fanatic friend, Alexis, with whom I never shared the same taste in men, said that he was fine. Picture him, 6' 2" tall, 240 pounds, muscular build, well defined arms, butter toffee complexion, the most intense medium brown eyes you could ever get lost in. His features were well defined. He could have graced the cover of GQ, Today's Black Man, any of the popular periodicals. He had a charm beyond words; charisma. I think the biggest thing about him that I could not get past was how well put together he was. Here he was at the prime of life, 36 years old, had a good job, a gorgeous split-foyer house with a swimming pool in an affluent section of PG County, MD, a 2002 Jeep Grand Cherokee, a 2003 Nissan Maxima – both paid for, he owned horses that he raced and frequently won with, he was so good to look at, when we would go out – he never pretended to leave his wallet at home, he just made me feel good in a way that no one else ever had. I was so used to busters, pimps, and clowns. I didn't know how to contain myself in the presence of what I thought at the time was a real man. But the signs were still there and I did not heed the warnings. My birthday came and I saw a little pink box on the kitchen counter, I just knew he had gotten me something nice. When I flipped it over it turned out to be a sample of something that came in the mail. We did go out to dinner later that day. Maybe I just expected more and I shouldn't have. But when Christmas came around, I gave him exactly what he asked for, a pricey set of books from Borders. What did he give me? Absolutely nothing! Nothing, you hear me? We had wild passionate sex most of the day, but that's no gift, we would do that anytime. Not a greeting card, not a thoughtful gift, and certainly not even a measly $50 gift card to Victoria's Secret. For as long as he had known me, he knew what I liked. I think he ignored me to see if he could start a fight and be done with me, but I didn't let him off that easily. I never said anything. I should have, I know I should have, but I didn't. It wasn't worth it to me. As low as my self esteem had gotten at that point, I wasn't feeling very worthy. I mean I had been struggling with why a man who has all he has going for him would want me. I'm not bad looking, I have a decent job, but I don't bring the bling. I couldn't buy a man, not that I would want to, but my resources weren't such that I could go in on a million dollar or more house with a person like this other woman from the dream that he was secretly entertaining behind my back, in real life, evidently could. She was a Hiring Recruiter for the Federal

Government, a "big wig". I was a lowly peon worker. But that still didn't justify him doing me the way he did. She would resurface later.

Maybe Christmas was such a big deal to me because I had just lost a baby right before the holiday. I was maybe 13 weeks pregnant. I was stressed out. He didn't want any more children, but despite all of our most cautious efforts it still happened. I worried so much and stayed so stressed that one day I was at work and started feeling dizzy. My co-worker told me I looked pale and to sit down. I looked at myself in the little mirror on my desk and I looked gray. Next thing I knew I was sitting in a puddle of blood. Another co-worker called 911 and in what seemed like 30 seconds, I was being whisked away to GW Hospital. My co-worker called Javier for me, but he claimed he couldn't get off from work to be with me. After about 2 hours, I had lost the baby and was being put under for a D & C. Because of the abnormal hemorrhaging, my doctor had me admitted. Though I spent the night in the hospital and cried for 24 hours straight, Javier was of no comfort. He didn't even come to get me when I was released the next day. Camille came and sat with me the whole night. When I woke up the next morning she was sitting right there at the foot of my bed with her arms folded, resting her head on the blanket folded by the TV tray. What would I do without her? None of my other friends came when they heard of the tragedy. Cassie was in a judgmental state, she didn't like the fact I was pregnant by Javier, how he was treating me cold because he didn't want any more kids, and the fact that we weren't married. Alexis doesn't drive and had to keep an eye on her teenage daughter, Alayna doesn't drive either so she couldn't get there. Camille came through like a true soldier for me and stayed by my side the whole time. When Camille took me home, Javier called me. He was just getting off a double shift from a terrorism threat and had the nerve to ask me, "So, you feeling ok?" That BASTARD! Of course, I didn't leave him alone at that point. I had to stick around for a while longer until I was ready to wipe the word "DOORMAT" off of my forehead. Javier lured me into his gravitational pull of charming deceit, but he was no less dark-hearted than my ex-husband Erick was to me over the course of our marriage.

THE GIFT

At fifteen years old I knew I was different, I saw things other people didn't see. I could relate to movies like Poltergeist and The Exorcist, but things like Freddy Krueger scared me too much to watch. I would have experiences in my mind before they happened and see things happen before they happened. I remember my first distinct vision, I was thirsty and put off going to the kitchen for fear I would open the cabinet and one of my father's prized glasses would fall out, crashing to the floor. I couldn't hold out much longer, I thought I was going to dry out from the inside out and I took a deep breath and headed into the kitchen. I carefully reached up and slowly opened the cabinet. Before I could reach up for a glass, one of the smoke colored juice glasses literally jumped off the shelf and hit the floor. It was as though someone pushed it from the back of the cabinet, just as I had seen in the vision. I wasn't wise enough to harness the power then. I didn't know how to control it. But as the years progressed, I learned how to use the signs, heed the warnings, and interpret dreams and visions. I had gotten to a point that I felt like my gift worked on everyone else but me. I just didn't always live in my prophecy like I should have, especially when it came to men, particularly Javier.

I remember an incident where one of my best friends, Camille, was having issues with her husband, Larry. Larry would barely work. The only time he had a job was when Camille got it for him (did the application, sent the résumé, etc.) Well, old Larry had gone and gotten himself a fancy car for someone so broke. Camille called me in tears, "I don't know how we are going to make it, Larry knows we are struggling to keep our heads above water, he has only been working for 3 months, and then he goes out here and does this!" I asked her, "Does what?" Camille took a deep breath and sighed, "He got a car, an Infiniti Q45." I cut her off before she could say anymore. Mind you, Camille and her husband lived in Calvert County which was a long way from my home in NE, DC. There was no way for me to have seen him with the car. I came straight home from work and had not been back out, but I burst out to her, "Is it burgundy with a tan interior?" She said, "Yeah, how did you know?" I said to her, "Girl, dry your tears up, this car is not going to be a problem, and he is not going to have it for very long!" Camille didn't seem to be at much ease with my prophecy, but exactly 3 weeks and 1 day later, she called me, "Hey, you were right! The dealer called Larry and told him to bring the car back. He had lied on the application about his income and they decided to renege on his financing. He took it this morning." I scared myself with this vision and the hundreds more that came over the years, but somehow, I was in 100% denial when the visions and messages and signs came about Javier, and even some of the warnings about Erick.

LET ME GIVE A LITTLE BIT OF HISTORY…

There is something much I don't like to talk about; the time when, I was married, to not only a client, but the "PLAYER'S CLUB PRESIDENT." I had fallen in love with him in high school. His name was Erick London. He went away to Morehouse College; I went to Valparaiso University in Indiana, only because they offered me a full ride on a scholarship. We both graduated and came back to the DC area. I had run into his friend from the neighborhood, Orlando. Orlando evidently called Erick and he went by my Aunt Lena's house, next door to where his grandmother used to live when we were in high school. Aunt Lena called me and told me this "dude" was looking for me and asked me if I wanted to talk to him. When she said it was Erick, I was relieved. I thought it would be Ralph, the lady-bug looking dork who was so in love with me in high school. I couldn't avoid Ralph, he lived on my block, he always had at least one class with me each year of junior high school, and he was everywhere I went. He was like MasterCard, everywhere you want to be - just harder to look at. I told her I'd call Erick. That was the beginning of the end.

It was the summer that I was 22 going on 23. Erick began taking me out, showing me a good time and all kinds of interest. It's a shame I didn't do more homework on him. His grandmother was a real religious soul. She cooked every day, cleaned, babysat for the neighborhood kids, and went to

9

church every single Sunday, rain or shine. His parents on the other hand were a different story. His mother was in jail doing 25 to life for stabbing her 3rd husband one hundred and three times. This happened the year Erick and I finished Archbishop Carroll High School. His father was in a psych ward up in NY somewhere. He had done so many drugs that he "retarded" himself. He had the mind of a 5 year old. He could no longer read and write. He could feed himself and use the bathroom freely, but nothing else. Erick went to Archbishop Carroll on a full scholarship. My Aunt Lena paid for me to go in the 12th grade, 1989-1990, when girls were first being admitted. She and Uncle Jason had hit the lottery for $100K, about $75K after taxes. They didn't want for much. Uncle Jason's parents had let them have their house on Alaska Avenue, NW when his grandfather died in 1970. They've been there, mortgage free, ever since. This $75K just enabled her to reach out and help those who needed it. Her only son was killed in the Gulf War in 1994 and her only daughter lost her life to cancer in 1987. My mother and Aunt Lena fought like cats and dogs when it came to her doing for me, but Aunt Lena insisted on the best for me. That's why she was so leery of telling me Erick was inquiring about me. I mean, Erick came out of school with a degree in Accounting and a minor in Business Administration, but he didn't make the wisest job choices. It was as though he thought the job would fall out the sky into his lap. He started out Auditing for Giant Food when he came home from Morehouse, the summer of 1994. They were paying him decent wages, maybe about $25K, which was good for the moment. I had my degree in Public Affairs with a minor in Fashion Design. I was managing a Fashion Bug for a measly $17, 500 a year and working on the design team for the now defunct Muriel's Boutique of Silver Spring, MD. I decided enough was enough and the market was too tight for my background and I took a few refresher courses from Trinity College in Public Affairs and Business Ethics, to try to get an edge. I landed a job with the law firm of Essex, Maddox, Sussex, and Winthrop LLP. The pay was great; I came in the door making $28K. In 1994 that was a good deal for a fresh college graduate. Erick and I continued to date seriously. On New Year's Day 1995 he asked me to marry him.

THE BEGINNING OF THE END

I came home from work one day after pulling a 12 hour shift on a campaign for the firm's new pre-paid legal service. I was bushed. I was so tired that I slept through two alarms the next morning. By this time Erick and I had moved in together into a one bedroom apartment on 11th Street, NW in DC. He nudged me as he was preparing to leave out the door. I didn't budge. He went in the bathroom and wet a wash cloth and dabbed my face with it until I came around. He looked at me, "Boo, you don't look too good, maybe you should call in today." I told him I couldn't, the campaign wasn't finished and I had 2 more days before the "Winter Hiatus" as we called it. That is when the partners gave everyone a 5 day weekend and shut the firm down. I got up, got in the shower, and got right out. I threw up so violently, like a scene from the Exorcist. I got back in the shower when I was done, brushed my teeth, dressed and headed out the door, against Erick's better advice.

When I got to work, everything set my stomach off. My co-worker had on Elizabeth Taylor's White Diamonds. I took off running for the bathroom, just to throw up much of nothing. Then the errand guy came back with lox and bagels. The salmon set my stomach off again. To the bathroom I raced. My supervisor came in behind me. She said to me, "Mandy, you look awful, do you think you have the flu? I just sent Kelsey and Baylor home an hour ago for the same symptoms you're having. Go home! I won't charge you leave for today and tomorrow. The campaign is just about done and I can take it from here. Do you need me to call someone for you?" I looked at her and told her I would be ok, that I would take a cab. I called Erick and told him I was going to see Dr. Wiseman because I didn't feel like I had a fever, but two of my co-workers went home in less than an hour before me with the same flu symptoms. He said he would meet me there because he had two hours before he had to be in a meeting and Dr. Wiseman was right on his block by the Giant.

I headed in to Dr. Wiseman's office feeling like the floor was coming up to meet me. I was so hungry and so nauseous at the same time. I asked the medical clerk at the window if it would be long before he saw me and she said he had one patient before me and then I would be next. It seemed like an eternity. I had my head resting in Erick's lap, he was stroking my hair and assuring me I would be ok. Finally, after what seemed to be an eternity, but was only 15 minutes, Dr. Wiseman came to the door and told me to come back to room 2.

Dr. Wiseman looked at me and asked me what I was feeling and what was going on with me. I told him I was vomiting violently. I was hungry and couldn't keep anything down. I kept feeling tired, no matter how much rest I got. He looked at me and said, "Miss Mandy, we're going to run a full chemical panel on you and a blood test for pregnancy." My eyes got wide as saucers and I hopped off the table, "Pregnancy? What? Not me, I'm too careful, this can't be, do you really think…" Then he cut me off, "It is just a precaution. It could just be a bug, but you have no fever, that is what makes me suspicious." I left the office a nervous wreck. I didn't tell Erick a word, I just had him drop me off at home and I got in my car and went to the drugstore. I bought two pregnancy tests.

I could barely get home fast enough. I was taking yellow lights left and right. I finally got in the door and made a mad B-line to the bathroom. I peed in a little bathroom paper cup and dipped the first test stick, put the cap on, and sat it on the counter. I tore open the second test, dipped the test stick in the cup, and put the cover back on that one. I poured the pee in the toilet and threw away the cup. In 5 minutes I had 2 lines on the first test. In

7 minutes I had two pluses on the other. I was pregnant. But how pregnant was I?

Erick came home from work that evening and I had left the two tests on the counter in the bathroom. I wasn't sure how he would react, but I was too tired to pack them up, throw them away, or do anything else. He came back to the bedroom and took off his shoes. He sat on the bed and asked, "You feel any better?" I just looked at him and pointed at the bathroom. He asked, "What, you want to go to the bathroom?" I mustered up the strength to say, "No, you comedian, go look in the bathroom." Erick slowly pushed the door open and peeked in. At first he didn't see anything; he then looked at the sink counter. I didn't hear anything, I waited a moment, I sat up, I walked into the bathroom and he hugged me so tight I thought he would pop one of my eyes out. He was ecstatic.

In the weeks that followed, Dr. Wiseman had me going to Dr. Harrison to be my obstetrician. At week 12 I had a sonogram and found that I was not having one baby, but 2. I passed out. 2 babies? I was just coming to terms with the fact I was pregnant. I wasn't married yet, I wasn't sure what Erick's true angle was with me, and now this. I told Erick that I had gotten so wrapped up in that pre-paid legal campaign that I neglected to notice that I hadn't seen a period in two months! Here we were facing Valentine's Day and I was too miserable to even enjoy a piece of chocolate candy. Erick handed me a box. I opened it and there was a nice little diamond ring in there. Keyword: LITTLE. I know it is supposed to be the thought that counts, but at this point I was learning how bad he really was with money. Nonetheless, he asked me to marry him in January but he announced to me right then, very excitedly, that the wedding day should be Valentine's Day and of course, I said yes and we did get hitched at the Justice of the Peace. No cake, no dress, just the certificate, the judge, his law clerk as a witness, and the couple waiting to be next. I was Mrs. Erick London, Mandy London.

August 22, 1995 rolled around and I gave birth to twin boys, Caleb and Kalen London. Life was getting a little bit rough. I took off on maternity leave from the firm, knowing I had no intent of going back. It was a "dog eat dog" environment and after 12 months there, I was ready for something less stressful and with days less than 12-14 hours a piece. I had been applying to the Federal Government and I took a job offer from the

Department of Justice, ironically where I would end up getting involved with Javier. I did not return to the law firm at the end of my maternity leave. I went straight into the Government. I worked from home for the law firm until the end of my contract, but I did not physically work in the firm.

RISE AND FALL - AUTUMN

On Monday, October 30, 1995, I walked on to my new job with DOJ as a Management Analyst. The building was in the downtown area of Washington, DC and at first glance it was overwhelming. On the first day, I had to go to the security office and get an official ID. There was a young man sitting outside the photographer's door. I was on a mission and barely noticed him in my peripheral vision, but he sure noticed me. "Eh hem, good morning to you too." I looked over at him as I headed for the photographer's door and basically gave a haphazard hello back to him. He said to me, "Why are you looking so mean? Did you get barked at for losing your ID or something?" I turned to him, slightly agitated at his persistent attempts at flirting and said, "And so what if I did?" He cracked a smile and said, "Are you always this serious?" I said to him in return, "Only when provoked", I then cracked a smile. He said, "I'm Javier." I looked at him and sarcastically said, "That's nice." I pushed the door open and went in to see the photographer.

I should have known I wouldn't be off the hook that easily. In the weeks to come, Javier kept crossing my path. I was still in the process of adjusting to being a new mother, things at home with Erick were getting tense, as I felt he wasn't pulling his weight in the finances or with the babies, and I was on the verge of being frazzled. The last thing I wanted to deal with was entertaining an attention starved pretty boy with his sights set on me. But somehow, something about Javier kept him on my mind.

One day, I was in the cafeteria on the lower level of the building when Javier came up behind me. I got my plate and headed into the dining room and he followed. This time I wasn't in the mood to resist him, so we sat for the entire lunch hour and had a good conversation. He said to me so many things that were so true. He said to me, "You put up a good front." I looked at him as if to say, "What the hell do you mean by that?" Before I could respond he continued, "You are not as happy as you want people to believe. You think there is more to life than where you currently exist, but you haven't grasped how to get there." I was beginning to be a little bit unnerved. Everything he said was right on the money. I looked at him and said, "Are you some kind of psychic, quasi prophet, warlock, or something?" He laughed at me, showing his near perfect teeth. He had that one little bit crooked tooth on the right side, but that made him even more distinct looking. I thought he was going to have a snappy come back, but he didn't. He just grinned at me and said, "I'm more like you than you think, and that is no come on line either. I've been married to Samantha for 7 years. We have two daughters. Serena is 7 and Alicia (Lish), is 18 months old. I knew this day would come one day, but I didn't know it would be last week. Samantha left and took the girls with her. The last two years of our marriage were a lie. I caught her so many times in compromising situations." I had to cut him off with a statement. "Were these situations following catching you compromising too?" He just looked at me and said, "No. I honored our vows. I moved Heaven and Hell for that woman. It was never good enough. Half the time she wouldn't work, I paid everything. I started betting on horses and winning, just to try to keep life nice for us. I know that sounds bad, I'm not a compulsive gambler, but it has really been difficult these last two years. When she said she was pregnant with Alicia, I was fit to be tied. I told her I hope she didn't think that would change things." With that, our hour was just about up. I stood up from the table and took my tray to the trash can. I told him we would finish this later and I walked away. I didn't know whether to believe him or not. Men always paint themselves as the saints that they aren't. There is always some sob story about a woman taking advantage of some good man somewhere. We never hear what it is that drives the behavior of these women, or what the men have contributed to the malfeasance. Half of the time, these men meander, they abuse women mentally or physically, they squander their money, or something. There is a root to it. Yet these alleged good guys never paint themselves as having any flaws. I mean look at Javier, he's fine. He has a great sense of humor, he's charming. He could have any woman he wanted. Something had to be up. I didn't truly allow him into my world at this point. Although he was a very persistent and confident, handsome young man, I held my ground. I did enjoy the occasional lunch and conversations. In the months to come, I would find out more in depth, all that encompassed being Javier. I just wasn't ready to jump out of the frying pan into the fire. For this reason, it took a few more years before Javier broke through my wall of defense.

HOLIDAY TIME 1995

The Christmas season was upon us and I had gotten to the point with Erick that I was ready to put him out or leave on my own. In fact, I did leave for a week at Thanksgiving. I went to stay with my Grandmother, Grams, in Richmond for a few days. I needed the time to clear my head about some things and to have a little help with the twins. Grams lived in what I considered a castle. It had five bedrooms, three and a half baths, a half acre lot, two kitchens, a grand foyer, full basement, and a finished attic. I could go there and think and she loved being with the babies in the family. They kept her young. Richmond is only a two hour drive down Interstate 95 from DC. I always visited Grams on holidays and this particular year was no different.

I maintain that Grams was the one who passed the prophetic gene on to me. She would see things before they happened. If you gave her a scenario, she could tell you the exact outcome. If you wanted advice you went to Grams. Even when you didn't ask for it, Grams had plenty of extra advice to go around. I should have known I couldn't fool her this year. I pulled up in her back driveway, but this time Erick was not with me. Even before we got married, he would go with me to visit Grams on any given occasion. As I stated before, his folks were otherwise *occupied* and Grams was fond of him, even if she did insist that I could have made better life choices. But it wasn't Grams' thing to stand in the way of true love or life's lessons. She always told me, "We all have our own life's lessons to learn, you make your mistakes. Lord knows I've made mine!" Grams had a sense of humor like no other, always a funny grandmother. We still laugh to this day about one time in her car when I was ten years old and she kept going on and on with a point like no one else could. She said to me, "I'm your grandmother, you're not my grandmother." But she couldn't let it rest there. She had to reiterate her point again. So I sat there. I just listened. Ten minutes later when I thought we were well beyond whatever it was, she looked over at me and with extra emphasis she said, "Don't you forget it, YOU'RE MY GRANDMOTHER, I'M NOT YOUR GRANDMOTHER." Then she looked at me again and we both burst into laughter. She couldn't let go the point and the third time she got it backwards and had to laugh at herself. This was the kind of fun amid seriousness we had all the time.

The day before I left Grams' house, she said to me, "The twins are sleep, come have some tea with me in the sunroom." UH OH! I knew it was serious. Anytime Grams pulled out the English Tea Service, it was serious. When Pop-Pop found out he had colon cancer and it had metastasized, she pulled out the tea set and had me and my Pops sit down to tell us the news. Pops was Grams' oldest son. She had another son, Philip, and my twin aunts Kristina and Lena. When the neighbor caught Aunt Kristina's husband tip-toeing out of a noted crack house, Grams, once again, pulled out the English Tea Service. I knew this had to be big.

"Sit down here Mandy," she said to me, peeping over her reading glasses as they hung over the edge of her nose. "I know you know the gift I have can be a blessing and a curse and that it isn't always easy to tell people things, even when I've been instructed by GOD, but I can't procrastinate anymore." I couldn't take the anticipation, "GRAMS what, you aren't dying are you? I can't handle another tragedy." She smacked her hand down on the table, rattling the tea pot, "HUSH and let me finish gal! Nobody is dying, but something worse will happen should you not let me get this out. Erick is not as responsible as you think he is. When you go home, gather up all of his bank statements, including that joint account you have together, the one I told you not to open, and the credit card bills. If you continue to have sex with him, protect yourself at all costs." She paused for a minute as if she knew I wanted to say something. "Grams, may I interject now?" I had to ask permission to speak. When Grams gets in her spiritual mode, it is best to not interrupt. She knew what I was about to say, but I said it anyway. "You want me to snoop behind Erick? I trust him." Grams took the reading glasses off and grabbed my hand with the death grip of any Kung-Fu Master, "LISTEN TO ME GAL! You don't know it all. Love will make you do things drugs can't! Listen and listen good! Loving Erick and being blind to reality will do nothing but get you hemmed up. He's not living up to his responsibilities with you, the babies, or your house. The biggest speech I have ever given you about him was to make sure he brings his money home. I know you are juggling more than your fair share. Erick is not a totally bad guy, but he will bring you down. The Titanic didn't need an anchor to keep it on the ocean floor. Girl you are about to hit that iceberg and he's becoming that anchor. You've been married all of 15 minutes and look at you, you're a walking wreck." Tears began to well up in my eyes and Grams came around the table and hugged me. "It's going to be alright baby. Just open your eyes."

HOMEWARD BOUND

Well the day came that I had to leave Grams' compound and return to real life. Erick was not home when I got there, I had no idea where he had been. The bed was made-up, pretty much the way I left it when I left for Richmond. The sink was empty in the kitchen and none of the groceries seemed to have moved. Where the hell had Erick been while I was away? The phone rang and I picked it up. It was Erick calling from his cell phone. "Hey BOO, you back home?" I said, "Um yeah, it's where you called me, isn't it?" "Right, right. How's Grams? The babies ok?" I sighed, "Everyone is fine, where the hell are you?" He paused a minute. "I'm at work, why?" I took a second to gather myself. I responded, "OK, well I'll see you when you get home. Please bring some wipes, we are about to be out." I knew I had a little time and I had to move fast. The doorbell rang. It was Cassie! Perfect timing! Alexis was getting out of the car with her. We had a big group hug and then I told them about my visit with Grams. Cassie took one twin, Alexis took the other and I was ready to go to work. Just then I heard a horn honk outside. I looked out and it was Collette. I couldn't believe it. Collette, who I had not seen in months, showed up. I asked Alexis and Cassie if they called her, both pled the 5th, but I knew. When Collette got to the door, I pulled her in by the hand and locked the door behind her. I said, "Girl, we got work to do!" We proceeded to go through Erick's desk drawer and sorted all of the bills by date, bank statements by quarter, and miscellaneous receipts by amount. Collette stumbled upon a MasterCard statement that she seemed apprehensive about letting me see. I reached behind her back and grabbed at it. She was insisting, "Now calm down, calm down. I don't want you to have an aneurysm when you see this." Oh mercy, what could it be? She handed me the bill.

The itemization blew my mind:

$ 217.39	Pleasure Palace Adult Entertainment/Toy Store
$ 102.50	Regal Royal Downtown Motel, Lovers' Special
$ 499.45	Kay Jewelers, Bracelet, Chain
$ 107.00	Enterprise Weekend Special Mid-Size Rental
$ 60.00	Nicholette's Hair Carnival & Day Spa Salon

I couldn't believe it. I didn't even remember to look at the dates. I slid down the wall to the floor. Alexis and Cassie had gotten the twins down for a nap just in time to see my melt down. "Grams was right. That bastard is cheating on me and has been for some time." I started to sob, Cassie and Collette hugged me for comfort, and Alexis ran for the tissues. At this point Collette stepped in and said, "You know what we have to do?" I had no idea what she was thinking. She blurted out, "Come on girl, it's time for a road trip to Kinko's. You are going to need a copy of all of this for your divorce proceedings." Damn! I hadn't been married a good year yet and it's over in my mind. Before we left Alexis pulled me to the side. She said, "You know my nosey *Betty-Housekeeper* nature, how I find things because I am so diligent with the housework - right?" I said, "Yeah, what did you do now?" She hesitated before pulling her hand out from behind her back, "I don't remember you being a size 16 ever." She then took both hands and extended a pair of large women's satin draws and a satellite dish of a bra that she found under the bed. I asked, "Where did you conclude the size 16?" She picked up some Lane Bryant brand name jeans with the 16W marked on the label. I was like, "DAMN, DAMN, DAMN", Alexis said to me, "Okay Florida Evans, let's get to Kinko's. Time is wasting." With that we left Cassie with the babies. Collette rode with us on our caper. It was actually a quick caper; we were done in less than 20 minutes. This allowed us the time to put everything back the way it was and be gone when Erick should have been returning home.

It was getting late and there was still no sign of Erick. This was odd for a Saturday. I called his cell and got no answer. His cousin DaJuan had called the house looking for him. I told him I had not seen him. DaJuan slipped and told me Erick had mentioned going by Aunt Felicity's house to pick up a letter for his mother to read next time he went to visit her in jail. Cassie, Collette, and Alexis were reading my mind. I called up Aunt Lena and asked her if she would watch the twins. She was more than glad to oblige without question. I packed their bag quickly; we dropped them off, and headed on a little venture to Aunt Felicity's house in Landover, MD. I must have broken a speed record, because a 20-25 minute trip took what seemed to be 10 minutes or less. We parked around the corner. I saw his 1990 Honda Accord behind the house. I saw another car I didn't recognize. It was a White Geo Metro. I didn't see Aunt Felicity's Volvo Station Wagon or her husband's Lincoln Town Car. I knocked on the door but no one answered. All I could hear was a stereo blasting kind of loud from upstairs. I turned the knob, and lo and behold, the door just mystically opened! I motioned for Cassie, Collette and Alexis to join me. They tipped up the walkway and followed me in. I could hear conversation in the distance, or what I thought was conversation, and then a loud yell. "OH ERICK, don't stop, don't stop, right there, OH ERICK!!!" Collette looked at me and said, "OH HELLS NO!" And went to charge up the steps, but Alexis pulled her back. Collette was furious. Cassie was a little bit bothered too, but she said, "We have to stay rational." With that I said, "I got your rational", and I charged up the steps and threw open the door to the back bedroom. When I opened the door, my jaw dropped to the floor. Collette pulled out the pocket camera and flashed about 4 good shots. He had some pregnant ho bent over the bed banging her brains out and both of them were butt naked. Embarrassed by being busted, he pulled out real quick, and I noticed he wasn't wearing a "cover", before he hurriedly stepped into his draws. I was beyond reproach, "What the F#@*ing HELL?" Erick was like, "Let me explain, it isn't what you think." I said, "Oh yeah? I think you were f#@*ing this b@#%h, that's what I think." He said, "Ok, I see how you could say that." Collette pulled me back, I was about to scratch his eyes out. Alexis reached in and pulled me down the steps. I heard the pregnant ho yelling at him, that he had told her he was done with me and it was over. I broke free from my girls and headed back up there, I said, "B@#%h, this is between me and him and unless you are ready to go into labor now, I suggest you take your pregnant ass up out of here. This is my husband you are f#@*ing, and unless you also want to pick up where we are leaving off the day you come out of the hospital, I suggest you gets to getting!" She hurriedly threw her slip-on dress over her big head and grabbed her shoes and dashed down the steps and out of the house. She didn't even grab her purse. I saw it on the chair and opened it. I read her student ID. This heifer just turned 16. She was a high school Junior at Landover High School. I didn't want to know, but I had some questions to ask. Collette interrupted me before I could say anything. "Is this how you treat the mother of your sons, your wife, and your life partner? That was a big b@#%h. I know whose parachute bloomers and size 16 tent jeans we found in the house now." Erick looked surprised. Alexis, who is the Evangelist of the group even interjected, "Hell hath no fury like a woman scorned. That's right, Turkey, we found the draws and the 54J satellite dish bra today." Cassie threw her hands up and said, "Hold it now, we're overlooking the obvious. That is probably his baby that girl is carrying." Needless to say, we left. I went home and called Aunt Lena. She said I could come and stay with her as long as I needed to. I started to pack and then I realized I wasn't the one in the wrong. With that I put my things back and packed up everything that belonged to Erick. He kept calling the house. I kept hanging up. The last time he called, I answered and told him he needed to come get his stuff off the sidewalk because at 6:30pm it was all going out on the sidewalk. I packed up his CDs, rather, all the ones I didn't want, his movies, his clothes, that big heifer's clothes, pictures, knick knacks, etc. I even took the stereo down. I called Mr. Barnsworth, the handyman for the building, and told him my key wouldn't turn in the lock. He came right up and put in a new cylinder. That solved that.

6:15pm came around and the girls had helped mè to line up all of his stuff at the door. We were counting the minutes. At exactly 6:29pm, Erick pulled up in his cousin DaJuan's black Suburban. He stuck his key in the door but it did not turn. He had to knock. I peeped out the door before unlocking it. He pushed the door in and proceeded to rush me like he was going to attack me. Cassie, Collette, and Alexis emerged from the kitchen as if to say, "I wish you would." Erick retreated. DaJuan came in and the two of them packed everything into the back of the Suburban. Erick didn't say two words to me. I had nothing to say to him, I was just relieved that he was leaving. Grams was right. I should have been a little bit less trusting and done my research in advance. I called Grams on the phone and she answered. Before I could get two words out, she said, "I know." Aunt Lena called behind my conversation with Grams and said she thought that the boys and I needed to come spend at least the night with her. Cassie, Collette, and Alexis helped me grab a few things and off to Aunt Lena's house I went.

10 STEPS TOWARD RECOVERY

A few days had passed since the incident with Erick and the pregnant cow. He had not called or tried to contact me or even inquired about the babies. I can't say I was surprised by this. I realized I had one month left to the lease and I paid it and gave the rental company my notice. I was going to move into another apartment, but Aunt Lena insisted on us staying with her until I could get my head together. I had been through a lot. I took a few days off from work. I had to put things into perspective. It was no longer just me, but the three of us that I had to be responsible for. Oh yeah, I made good money, but single parenting is always hard.

I went back to work and had a hard time keeping the tears out of my eyes. This whole situation was devastating. The man I loved more than words could express thought so little of me as to have an affair for GOD only knows how long. My world was crumbling around me. All I had was my friends, the babies, and Aunt Lena. Javier tried his best to approach me at work, out of what he considered concern, but there was nothing a man could say or do for me at this particular point. I was inconsolable. I was in a crowd, but so alone.

One of my first major steps was to go to court and file papers for child support. In DC, at that time, you had to be separated for 6 months before you could file for divorce. I had a couple more months to go at this point, but I was still given a court date. Erick was served his notice at his Aunt Felicity's house, his refuge from the world. We both showed up for court when the date came up. Erick's harlot had the baby already and he tried to use that as a reason he couldn't pay but so much in child support, even though he didn't think the child was his. The court ordered him to have a paternity test on the other child before any consideration would be given in a lower amount. Erick complied. Guess what? The baby **was** his and the judge did not consider a reduction in payments as a result! He had taken up with this high school girl, persuaded Aunt Felicity to let her move in with him into her house like she was just a charity case he was trying to help out, and the baby was his after all. Here's the kicker: Erick was too embarrassed to abandon her at this point. He felt as though he had ruined the chance he had with me and his first family, so he sought redemption with this girl, like she was his second chance; the chance he needed to redeem himself and try to convince the world or himself that he could be a responsible father.

Everything in life happens for a reason. Javier happened into my life and it was no accident. Likewise, Cassie's sudden crisis was the distraction I needed to take my mind off of my crumbling life. Just two weeks after my court situation, Cassie got a sudden phone call at work. Her mother had a stroke and was on her way to the operating room for immediate surgery. I told my supervisor I had an emergency and needed to go and then I called Collette and told her the situation as I left for the hospital. Let me just paint you a visual, not only did Cassie and her mother look exactly alike, they were closer than the Judds. Cassie and her mom were both short and stocky women. Her mom was a golden honey color, while Cassie was a little browner. Cassie's father was murdered when she and her 4 sisters were young. As a result, they became exceptionally close. She was the oldest of the 5 girls and became her mother's right hand. Ever since then, they have been more than mother and daughter, they have been best friends.

When I arrived at the hospital, the surgeon was in the hallway talking to Cassie. Collette said she would meet me there and she wasn't far behind me. When I got to the waiting area, I dashed over to Cassie just in time to catch her on the way to hitting the floor. It was as though her knees gave out on her. The surgeon turned to walk away and as I guided her to the chair, I turned to ask him what he said to her. He just looked at me and said, "Something no loved one ever wants to hear." Mercy! What the hell does that mean? Cassie was sobbing uncontrollably. After about 5 minutes, Collette came into the waiting area where we were sitting. I hadn't been able to stabilize Cassie to say two words, but when she did, she muttered, "Why Lord? Why not take me instead?" We knew it was serious. A few more minutes passed, Collette and I were expecting the worst. The surgeon came back and told Cassie she could go "see" her mother. Collette and I stood in the hall, peeping in as people came out of the ICU. It was horrible. There lay Lola with all kinds of hoses and tubes attached to her. We couldn't go in, but we waited for Cassie to come out.

In the weeks to come, Cassie had to go through all of her mother's personal business to find out what kind of resources were available, short of selling her childhood home, to pay for the extended care. There was a minimal likelihood that Lola would ever regain full mobility, in fact, the doctors predicted only a 25% recovery. Although Lola and Cassie were close, there were a few secrets. When Cassie was going through her mother's papers, she found a bank statement for an account other than the checking they had together. They had the checking together to avoid hassles should a crisis like this arise, but this other account was new to Cassie. It seemed her mother had either hit the lottery or neglected to tell her or she had been laundering money for the mob. The most current statement read $12,000,000.00. At first, Cassie thought it was a mistake so she searched for more statements, the one before it was pretty much the same. Where did all this money come from? Why was it a secret? Surely Medicare would be looking to get their hands on it and Cassie would not have it!

Cassie did not want to raise a stink with the family, so she called her sister, the next in line, Maxine. Maxine was a CPA. She too was baffled at the money. Cassie and Maxine decided to keep this between just them. In the days that followed, strange letters came to Lola's house. Cassie began to get suspicious. Did her mother actually have a stroke or was it a cover up?

Friday night, Cassie came by my house. She told me what she was feeling and I didn't like the vibes I was picking up on. Of all times, that psychic prophecy thing would kick into overdrive! I had a vision. The company Lola was working for the last 30 some odd years was a front. I told Cassie, that money was from a secret, but I just couldn't figure out what. I tried to focus but I couldn't get it. I felt like I told her too much already. I was getting scared. Just as I was to the point I thought I was going to spaz out, the phone rang. I reached for it and knocked over the glass of grape juice I had on the coffee table. As I saw the grape juice creep across the table, it hit me that money was to keep a secret, something too heinous to talk about.

In the days that followed, Collette did a search on the internet for Hawkshaw Enterprises. Research is her life and if anyone can find something it's her! It seems that Hawkshaw Enterprises was a "shadow" corporation set up to look like a subsidiary of another company. In fact they had not existed for 30 years. Granted, Lola had told Cassie the company changed hands a few times over the years, she was hiding something nonetheless. Collette found where there were hidden assets, but the ownership of the company was unclear. She checked the Better Business Bureau and the Department of Commerce, there were no records. Cassie suddenly had a flashback about a locked box her mother kept, a fireproof safe. The key had to be somewhere logical so off I went, to meet Cassie at Lola's house. My Aunt Lena called me and said she would watch the twins. It was perfect timing.

Lola lived in a basic Cape Cod style house in the 4400 block of Illinois Avenue, NW. She had 4 bedrooms upstairs and a bathroom. Cassie knew the key would be in the 4th bedroom. That is where her mother kept everything important, centrally located for accessibility. After a quick sweep of the room she reached her hand under the desk and found the key. As if her feet could not reach the floor, she dashed down the steps to the hallway and raced back to the den. She carefully inserted the key in the locked box and it popped open. There was a black diary and a letter that looked like a legal contract. In opening the diary, she found it was her mother's handwriting spanning from September 1, 1977 to December 31, 1994. This was a big legal size ledger diary, like you use to sign in at a government building. It had to be about 500 pages thick and ran the length of the locked box. It's funny the things you remember when you find yourself in a situation like this. Cassie said to me, "You know, it's odd, there are 5 of us. I turned 5 the day Daddy died, and I only remember Mama going to the hospital once, and that was when I was two years old. She had Maxine.

Raven, Danielle, and Sasha just seemed to come home one day, one at a time. I don't remember Mama being fat or sick or anything after Maxine. I remember the day Daddy died, we all left our house in Connecticut to live in this one. I never heard from Mama J, Daddy's mother, again after the move. It was like Daddy's family disappeared and seemingly my nickname went away too. My mother used to call me Kirsty. All of a sudden, I went to school and everyone was calling me Cassie. Now that I think of it, we used to call Maxine 'Annie'. How do you get Cassie out of Kirsty and Maxine out of Annie?" Now I began to wonder about Cassie, was she cracking up or what? Cassie took the contract and the journal with her. I went home and immediately called Grams. After a few words she cut me off, "What is on your mind gal?" I told her, "Cassie…" and she cut me off again. She said, "I wasn't going to tell you and you must let her figure this out on her own. Remember when she moved into the neighborhood, you were about 5, I think you just had your birthday in August and she moved on the block about a month later? Well, she wasn't just moving here to start school. Her mother was in a witness protection program." I was dead silent. Grams said, "Did you hear me, you there girl?" I replied, "Yes Grams, I hear you." I said to her, "What happened?" Grams got silent and sighed, "Well there was a situation where your friend's mother saw something she shouldn't have seen. Also, the one sister is the only whole sister. I know you are saying that she has several, no – you know the one. The one close to her is the only whole sister." So I am sitting there like, "So who are the other three chicks? Did they really fall out the sky or what?" Then I asked Grams about Cassie's suspicions. "Grams, Cassie said she didn't remember her mother having Raven, Danielle or Sasha. They just appeared one day, one at a time. Could they be adopted?" Grams said to me, "Nope. They have to do with the situation. They are not Lola's children, but they are related to Cassie and Annie." I asked Grams how she knew Maxine's alter ego. She just chuckled at me and said, "Don't you know by now? It's the gift, so don't do nothing you will be ashamed for me to tell you." With that I hung up and went to bed.

The next morning, Cassie called me. She had been up all night reading that journal. She said to me, "Mandy, my real name was Kirsty and Maxine was Anastasia. That's why we called her Annie. Mama took the money and Daddy's three extramarital kids in exchange for our lives. Daddy insisted on bringing them home one at a time, literally one at a time three days in a row. Then he met his demise. I remember feeling like I didn't have a birthday that year, like everyone forgot me. Everything happened so fast. My whole life has been a lie. That house was bought with hush money. The witness relocation program gave me, Ma, and Maxine new identities." I could see the tears welling up in her eyes and we were just on the phone. Suddenly Erick and the drama of my life began to pale in comparison.

30 days had passed since the stroke. Lola was hanging on by threads. At 2:12am on a Saturday morning, she passed. Cassie was at her side. The doctors had called her and told her that the time was near and she camped out for the duration the night before. Cassie had found her mother's will. She had left the money, whatever was left of it, to Cassie and Maxine. Cassie was in shock and when everything cleared, she gave me $500,000. I tried to not accept it, but she insisted. She told me I had been too good of a friend to her over the years. She gave Alexis and Collette $250,000 each. I never told them how much I got. I needed it. I should have made a fresh start but I was apprehensive. I paid to have the Victorian farmhouse on my farm on Route 721 in King and Queen County, VA restored, so that I could have my own place to stay, close to Grams. The cash helped me to get through a rough time and take care of bills I couldn't on just my salary and with Erick's lack of support. I really got on my feet, but not up enough to save myself the Javier heartache.

TIME GOES ON

Six months had passed since Lola's death. The estate probated at record speed, I've never seen anything like it. On a peaceful Friday night, Cassie, Maxine and I were sitting in the den at Lola's house (Cassie and Maxine decided not to sell it), reminiscing on a few of the good times growing up in the neighborhood. Then came a forceful knock on the door. There were no lights on at the front of the house, so Cassie tipped to the door and peeped out the peephole. Just as she was peeping, another forceful knock came and she dashed back to the den. She could hear men outside talking, but couldn't make out what they were saying. After what was considered a safe amount of time had passed, Cassie opened the door. There was a note. It read: "Vinnzio Vincenzi of the Banotti Cartel was here. We will be back." Gracious! What on earth was that about? We were all unnerved. I called my good buddy, Lieutenant Grayson, over at 4D and told him the situation. He also grew up in the hood with us and we all kept in touch. He used to tell me that if I ever needed anything, just call him. This was the time.

Grayson answered the page I sent to him in less than 5 minutes. I put Cassie on the phone and let her tell him what was up. He sent over 2 squad cars – 4 officers total. They searched the perimeter, the front and back yard, up and down the block, the basement, the whole house. One of the officers noticed a suspicious looking car at the end of the block. When he and his partner approached, it took off, but not without them getting the tag numbers. Grayson called back over to Lola's house and told Cassie and Maxine to clear out. Just before we were about to leave, one of the other officers found something suspicious by the back basement door. It looked as though someone had contemplated breaking and entering. Although there was an iron gate, there was a crowbar on the ground and a set of bolt cutters up under the porch steps. Maxine set the alarm, and we left the premises.

In the days that followed, Lola's neighbors called Cassie and told her about strange happenings. Mrs. Jennings called from the house on the right and told Cassie that two men resembling the "Men in Black" knocked on her door and asked her and her husband a bunch of questions about how well they knew Lola and showed pictures of some people that may have come and gone over the past year or so. Mr. Foster called from the house on the right. He said that he kept seeing this same vehicle parked in front of the house all night, several nights in a row, and then it just stopped. Maxine, being the fire engine that she can be at times, took it upon herself to go over to Lola's house alone, to pick up the mail. When she turned the key in the lock and opened the door, she dashed over to the ADT alarm box only to find it wasn't engaged. Terrified, knowing that she and Cassie made sure it was set the last time they were there, she grabbed up the mail, slammed the door shut, and dashed out toward her car. Just as she hit the sidewalk and was about to dash down the block to her car, it exploded. Maxine fell to the ground, but wasn't hurt. She grabbed her cell phone out of her pocket and called 911. Mr. Foster came running out of his house and picked her up off the ground and took her in. A few moments later the fire trucks reached the scene.

Mr. Foster called Cassie on her cell phone and told her not to come, no matter what. Maxine then told Mr. Foster to call Lieutenant Grayson for her and tell him what happened. As they were on the phone, 3 police cars pulled onto the scene and blocked off the entire block at both ends with yellow tape. Cassie was frantic. She called me and told me what happened. I told her to get off the phone and call Maxine back. If there were any clues to this, they had to be in the mail she gathered out of the house before the car blew up. Maxine had put the mail in her purse and had that on her shoulder as Mr. Foster pulled her to safety. She opened the purse and found a brown envelope with no return address. Nervous and shaking, Mr. Foster took the letter from her and cut the end off with scissors. There were pictures of her mother, Lola, fraternizing with several unidentified men, holding drinks, having the best of times. These guys didn't look like the typical Mafia type. They were handsome black men. Ok FINE black men. On the back of one of the pictures there was a post-it note saying, "Some accidents happen on purpose, that's why some illnesses have no cure." It was the picture of Lola holding an Apple Martini. Lola was not a true drinker, but she never turned down a good Apple Martini. Hmm, could this have been the cause of her stroke, green liquor in a glass? Looking closely, Maxine saw the sign in the back drop, "The Mauphisto." They were at the Mauphisto club in Georgetown. These pictures happened within days before Lola's stroke because Maxine could remember the day Lola got the heart pendant necklace she was wearing in the picture. Maxine gave the pictures to the officers along with the envelope. After opening all of the other mail, she did not find anything else shocking. No one else was hurt. Her car was the last one at the end of the block and only minimal damage was done by flying glass to a nearby Toyota. This could have been so much worse.

After a once over by the paramedics, Maxine was cleared. An officer took her to the 4th District Police Precinct (4D) where Cassie came to meet her. Cassie had the diary with her. She told Maxine that there was more to their lives than just changes in identity. Their mother was an informant for an underground Mafia style gang. The hush money was what was paid to her for keeping secrets and leaving the state of Connecticut where everything went down. Cassie's father's death had something to do with all of the scandal, but exactly what? Did it even matter? All I know is, everything that was bothering me, seemed so small at this point that I could no longer focus on my problems. I realized that they weren't significant.

THE JAVIER SAGA CONTINUES

We reach a point where we get tired of being alone, tired of being in a bad relationship when we know we deserve better. Sometimes our loneliness draws predators to us. These predators sense our vulnerability and take full advantage. I am now convinced that Javier was an opportunist pig. Looking back at the dream incident in his driveway with the AMAZON behemoth woman, I realize now that the signs were all there. An incident comes to mind where all I needed was a house to land on me over the course of the weekend, just to hit the point home. Javier's Aunt Flora was having a birthday party for her son Harold, who recently was released from prison. Harold was framed for a murder, based on circumstantial evidence. When the actual criminal had committed another crime, in which DNA linked him to several other offenses, it came out that he was also the trigger man and Harold was set free. I can't say that I would celebrate my thug son's prison release, I mean if he wasn't fraternizing with the wrong crowd he never would have been in a position to be pinpointed now would he? That is neither here nor there. The party was thrown one Saturday evening and all was going well. Aunt Flora had on her grandma-style bathing suit with the skirt around it and her matching rubber swim cap with the fake flowers. Several cousins were flailing about in the pool, splashing around playing volleyball with a big air filled beach ball, and others were just hanging around. It was late in the evening. The cake had been cut in celebration, and Javier's cell phone rang. He answered and then casually slid to the edge of the yard to talk with his back turned. 1st RED FLAG! After the call, I didn't dare ask if everything was ok. I just pretended to not notice. Later on, I went into the house as everyone was clearing out for the night. By this point it had to be about 1am. Sometimes, "our folks" just don't know how to leave. I remember heading upstairs to put some used towels in the hamper in the hall when I saw Javier's suitcase by the window. I remember that he had just come back from a two week training session out west. I went to grab the suitcase to put it in the closet, out of sight, when I noticed the airline tag on it had someone else's name on it. "CATRICE SIMMONS". Hmmm? I didn't give it another thought, I mean I have loaned out luggage before and gotten it back with tags on it. I know that the back of my subconscious was beginning to put two and two together. Sunday morning I got up. Javier made a hap-hazard attempt at an early morning "spoon". I wasn't feeling it. I wanted to ask so bad, "Who is Catrice Simmons?" But then I am sure it would have been a cousin or a neighbor or something stupid. I left it alone. After he got off of me, he fell back to sleep. I got out of bed, slipped on my swimsuit, and went for an early morning swim of my own. He finally got up and I came in the house, washed off all the chlorine, and got dressed. That was the last night I spent at his house before the AMAZON woman dream incident. Monday morning, Javier had called me up to his office to see if I could help him find a file he lost in his computer. He didn't want his supervisor to know he couldn't find the file, and classified information was my specialty so I agreed. He had me sit at his desk while he went to another computer to send over the second part of the files he lost. I was supposed to be finding the first part once I received the second part on his desk. It took forever for the second part to come. I saw his email notification pop up. It said, "2 new messages, Catrice Simmons". Hmmm. There is that name again. I told him that one file from the second part came but the other was missing, and to send it again. He did. As he was waiting across the room, I scrolled through his emails. I found what must have been dozens of emails spanning 6 months from Catrice Simmons. Almost all had been opened, but not deleted. Some just said basic things like "HI HONEY" and "YOUR LOVE HAS MEANT SO MUCH TO ME", there was some poetry, yet others were more elaborate, like the one with the floor plans to the house he showed me that he wanted to build. I wondered why he had a sudden interest in selling his house. I thought he wanted more room to make us one big family, his daughters and my sons. It seemed that this two week trip out west was actually a trip he took to New York City with Miss Catrice Simmons. They went to see some Broadway shows and a whole gamut of other interesting sights. After that trip, I noticed by date that the emails got more intense. She was telling him how much his love has made a difference in her life; there were email cards, more poetry, and more sentiments. She went on with how she looked so forward to marrying him the following June, after they finish building their house. Oh I couldn't take it. I had to stop. She works as a contractor for the government, as I said early on; she was doing well for herself. At first I wondered what made her better than me, but maybe that isn't the question to be asking. I found Javier's missing file. I showed it to him and I left without a word. I figured that if I brought up the emails, it would escalate into a serious battle, and I just didn't have the energy for that.

SO WHAT DO I DO NOW?

I had been through so much with this man: a lost baby, a miserable Christmas, his frequent travels for the job (if you can say that). I had just been through so much. And for him not to have the respect for me to say he wasn't feeling me anymore or maybe we need to take a break, but to rather use me for my stability and plan a life with another woman, that was just too much. Javier would call me and I wouldn't answer. If I answered, I was always in the middle of something, too busy to talk. After about two weeks of this, he came down to my office on a Friday. He was looking like a million bucks in a high end, well tailored suit. He told me that thanks to me finding his missing file he got a promotion and a cash award. It seems that old Javier finished his project in record time, because of me finding that file and him not having to reconstruct his work. Stupid me! Hoping that loving him as much as I did would make him love me back the same. I didn't say much and by this time he was beginning to feel my chill. Although we still worked in the same building, I didn't have to see him unless I made an effort. Whatever we had, it was clearly done, stick a fork in it! It was at this point I began seriously reevaluating my options for remaining in the Washington, DC Metro Area.

OPEN MOUTH, INSERT FOOT

I was sitting at the kitchen table in Aunt Lena's house, on a quiet Friday evening, contemplating my next move, when there was a knock at the door. It was Camille. I let her in and she grabbed a mug off the counter and poured some hot water for tea. She sat down with me at the table. She asked me if I had spoken to Alayna lately. I had to think for a second, in fact I had not. Alayna had also been a very good friend to me in the times that my "core girls" weren't there (Alexis, Collette, and Cassie). I had backed away from her about a year ago due to a misunderstanding at her house. It was Memorial Day. Alayna and I were sitting in the dining room having a conversation with Nana – Alayna's godmother. Some of Alayna's live-in boyfriend Richy's buddies from the hood came by to cookout with us. The baby's mama of one of the guys came in and sat in the living room. She didn't speak to us, didn't join our conversation, or do much else for that matter, but she brought her two "SCREAMING MEEMIES" into the house with her. They put Bay-Bay's kids to shame! At one point she got tired of the 2 year old trying to climb the stairs so she took her and held her between her knees until she started to squawk. The squawking escalated to squealing, then straight crying. I already had a migraine. I said to Alayna, "I wish she would keep that child quiet". I said it to Alayna, not the baby's mama, not anyone else. Evidently, the baby's mama heard me and got offended. She collected her little pick-a-ninnies and went outside and told Richy that I said a whole bunch of things I didn't say, and then she and the crowd of buddies all left the premises. Next came Richy to the door, motioning for Alayna. Alayna went out; Nana picked up on the tension and said something to the effect of them fighting. Next thing I know, I better leave. Alayna is telling me that this isn't my house and I shouldn't have said anything. Well, black people always want to throw something up in your face about something being their house whenever they get a chance so I said goodbye to Nana and I left. I didn't talk to Alayna for weeks after that. She finally called me and had the nerve to try to say I shouldn't let this incident come between our friendship. Say what? I was blown. Who was she talking to with her "Miss-this-is-my-house" self? Who? The same friend who drove her to the grocery store to keep that lazy sucker fed when he wouldn't work, only for him not to part his lips with a single word of thanks when he took the bags out of my trunk. Not a single word of hello or goodbye did he mutter to me, so who is letting what come between what? He beat her. I knew he did, because the last time I talked to her, maybe a month before, she was saying how bad she wanted him out of her house and he declared he wasn't going anywhere. That wasn't the distressing part. She told me how they were fighting so bad she sent her two kids to stay with her sister for a week. She was going to come stay with me, but I guess he threatened her and she backed out. I had been talking to Cassie about her. Cassie is our resident psychologist in the group even though she often needed one herself. Ironically, she studied it in college. She's the rational thinker and analyzer in the crew, most of the time. She even said Alayna is living in fear. It seems this guy had told her very graphically what he would do to her during one of their fights. I had forgotten that until Cassie reminded me. My memory was jogged again, while talking to Camille. Camille told me about one time she was at Alayna's house and it took her forever to come out so they could go to the mall. When she came out she had her shades on and wouldn't take them off for anything, even inside the mall, even when the sun went down on the way home. I know I had tried my best, along with Alayna's sister, Nana, and a couple of her other friends, to get her to go get a restraining order, but as Cassie put it, "The fear is stronger than her will right now." I worried about her kids. The boy was 17 and the girl was 16. They would go to jail if Richy killed their mother, they would take him out! My question was: what kind of message are you sending them about morals, relationships, and self respect? What kind of example are you setting for your kids to have in their own relationships?

Upon Camille's urging, I pushed the button on the speaker phone and called Alayna. There was no answer so we left a message. Camille went over to the small kitchen TV and turned it on. The local 6 o'clock news had just come on. The anchorwoman said, "We're recapping stories from the last hour in case you just tuned in. A woman was found beaten severely in her row house on 12th Street NE, we switch to Brad Brenner in the field", then the view switched to Alayna's block and my cell phone rang, it was Cassie. Sarcastically she retorted, "I'm looking at the news, isn't this house on 12th Street where our good friend Alayna lives?" I didn't want to hear that. I knew she was being sarcastic. Brad Brenner was giving a recap of the events, "Well it seems as though the young woman residing in this house didn't show up at work today. Two coworkers called when the supervisor said he had not heard from her. Getting no answer, one of the coworkers looked on the victim's desk in the Rolodex and found her sister's number. After contacting the sister, she left her job and went to the house. When there was no answer, but she could hear the TV going in the background very loud, she used her spare key to enter the residence where she found the victim sprawled out on the floor in the doorway between the dining room and kitchen." At this point the camera panned over to the police lieutenant on site who gave a statement, "We are in pursuit of a suspect at this time. We have some leads but no definite findings. We will not release names pending an actual arrest. We have reason to believe this was not a random act of violence or a robbery attempt." With that I turned the TV off and told Cassie I would call her back. Camille and I headed out the door and went to the police precinct. Camille was thinking what I was, where Richy might be. He had been fooling around with the mother of his 18 and 20 year old daughter and son behind Alayna's back. She lived in Lake Arbor off of Central Avenue. Camille and I had seen them together, having an intimate dinner at the Marriott at Metro Center when we were celebrating Collette's wedding. I told her about it, but she didn't seem fazed. Maybe she was too scared to say something to him. They had a room together there. We saw them. I guess sometimes it takes a house to land on you to make you deal with something. At the police station, we gave the desk sergeant the address of Richy's ex. We also gave them the address to a house he used to stay at with a bunch of his buddies, and the halfway house he stayed in when he first got out of jail, before he came to stay with Alayna, the bar he drinks at on Fridays and so on and so on. My cell phone rang while we were in the station, it was Nana. Alayna wasn't doing too well. They had her at Washington Hospital Center in the ICU. Nana said she had a broken eye-socket, two cracked ribs, internal bleeding and swelling of the brain. She was unconscious. The next 24-48 hours would be touch and go.

RICHY'S POORNESS

Well, leave it to the worst criminals to be the dumbest. At 2am in the morning, PG County Sheriff's Deputies knocked on the door of Richy's ex in Lake Arbor. Two officers covered the back. You could hear scuffling inside the house. After a few moments of no one answering the door, the officers kicked in the front door and stormed the house. An officer detained the ex, and two other officers found Richy in the closet of the master bedroom. Both were taken into custody. Kionshaye Langdon and Richard Wesley's lives would be forever altered. CSIs on the scene of Alayna's house found 3 sets of DNA, hers, Richy's and a third person. It appeared that Richy wasn't acting alone. None of this helped Alayna, but when daybreak came, I called Nana. I asked her where the kids were. She said they were with Alayna's older sister. They weren't coping with this too well. Her son vowed revenge. It's funny how things progress. Nana said that Alayna regained consciousness early in the morning, the swelling in her brain had been brought under control, and there was no reason to believe she wouldn't pull through just fine. There was no permanent brain damage nor was there any permanent damage to her internal organs. An officer that had been stationed outside her door came in and took a brief statement. She told him that Kionshaye came to the door early that morning and Richy let her in. An argument ensued about her being in the house. They argued all the way to the kitchen where Richy took a cast-iron skillet and banged her in the head. Kionshaye began hitting and kicking her when she fell and then blacked out completely.

Three weeks passed and Alayna was released to go stay with her sister. Richy and Kionshaye were both out on bond. Alayna's sister was worried that her son would go after both of them while they were out pending trial. It was the court's order for Kionshaye and Richy to stay in the vicinity and not have any contact with each other. In an odd and unfair twist of fate, Kionshaye sent Richy a text message on the day she was released, asking if she could meet him at the Largo Metro Station. Shortly after dark, she picked him up in her car and they got on Central Avenue heading to the beltway. As they entered the beltway, exiting the off-ramp, a tractor trailer lost control in the next lane, jack-knifed and capsized right on top of their car, crushing them to death instantly. The driver was not seriously injured, nor was he charged with reckless driving. "Vengeance is mine", said the Lord. That is exactly what it was. Though the demise seemed too easy for both of them, it saved Alayna's kids from doing something they would forever regret.

CAMILLE, IF YOU WILL...

Camille is a friend who came into my life at an unexpected time and in an unexpected way. I was taking a few refresher courses some years ago, and she was in two of them with me. We just bonded like we had been friends since kindergarten. When I first met her, she was married to the BAMA of the YEAR, Larry. I think it was her need for reassurance that drew her to me. I was the only one she talked to in those classes. I didn't really talk to anyone else but her either, for that matter. I think we complimented each other, her with her damaged will power and me with my damaged self esteem. We were like two broken dishes on display in a fancy China closet. Beautiful in the outside view, but chipped underneath. I can't say I have ever felt or detected a note of jealousy from her, and I certainly wasn't envious of all of her problems, but somehow, as the years progressed, I found myself sometimes wishing I had the magnetism for attention that she did. Don't get me wrong, I am no dog by any standard, I'm just not extremely curvaceous and don't don the "bang-py-yow" hips and junk in the trunk that she does. When we would go out, it seemed guys would always flock to her, as though I didn't exist. We went to Wal-Mart one Saturday afternoon and just going in the door these two guys approached her and were sweatin' her like she was Halle Berry or some celebrity. I was just like, "Ok are we going to shop, or have I stepped into the Miss America Pageant and won 3rd runner up and no one bothered to tell me?" For a minute, I think she was engulfed in the attention and ran with it. See, her liberation from Larry was a long time coming, but when the judge handed her the divorce papers, all of a sudden, her brokenness shifted. Mine took some time, plenty of work on self confidence, and makeovers, but she really stood out. I had to ask a non-biased guy (who did not know her), "What is it about her?" And he said to me, "In all honesty – YO – the first thing guys see is that long hair or *good hair*, as you refer to it, those *tig ol' bitties*, and that big ass." Well, at least he was honest. He still maintained that once you get past that, you get to know how a person really is, but that is the initial attraction. At that point I felt like Cinderella, sitting home while the wicked step sisters enjoyed the ball. I felt like such a frump. Guys that I would be drawn to and approach, would brush me off to try to "HOLLA" at her. Most of the time she would reject them, but on occasion, she would take one or two of them up on an offer of dinner or a movie. Often nothing came of it, but there was one guy, that I grew up with, who I would run into on occasion when I visited Aunt Lena. I always had a crush on him, ever since the 7th grade; Jonathan Daniel. I never would have expected that Camille and Jonathan would get together. Sometimes she would come to Aunt Lena's and we would cook out. Jonathan would come by and mingle with everyone in the yard. I never noticed him mingling more than usual with Camille. Camille usually tells me everything. Jonathan made me feel like he had an interest in me, at one point, now that I think about it –but nothing ever came of it.

One day, Camille and I were riding to Target or Wal-Mart or both, as we often did in our free time, and she said she wanted to talk to me about something. I asked, "What?" When she has to talk about something, it is usually something I don't know if I need or want to know about because it could drag me down. You know how some people dump their burdens on you and they walk away feeling better and you stand there wondering why you feel so bad all of a sudden, and the other person is now happy, jolly, and relieved? That's what it's like. She had been through so much with Larry stalking her after the divorce, I was worried that he had threatened her again or did something to try to harm her. Do you know what she said to me? She just blurted out, "Jonathan and I have been seeing each other for the last 6 months." Playing dumb I said to her, "Yeah, I know, at all of Aunt Lena's cookouts, cook-ins and card parties." She looked at me and said, "No, I mean see-ing each other." I was thinking, "I see said the blind man." I got quiet. I didn't know what reaction she expected. I was kinda nonchalant. I mean nothing happened between me and Jonathan; we talked a lot too, about a lot of things, never Camille though. We never talked about us having anything either, he was just a really good friend, a friend I had hoped would come after me – being single, eligible and as lucrative as he appeared to be. Oh well. I mean I wasn't all that blown away about it, all the men flock to her, like I said before. I mean, I guess I should have expected it right? Maybe she thought I would respond, "OH MY GOODNESS?!!!" In reality, I was just thinking, "OK." I don't know why she felt compelled to tell me that. Jonathan called me right after she told him she shared this tidbit with me. He didn't understand why she felt so compelled to tell me either. I mean, what was the point? Were we bragging or were we seeking approval? Were we reaching for shock value? I don't know what the point was, Jonathan didn't know what the point was, all I know is it didn't change much of anything. I still continued to be friends with her and him just like before, just now I really felt like the 3rd runner up for Miss America…

ALEXIS PUTS HER BUTT ON HER BACK FOR THE DAY

Alexis and I had been friends since the 7th grade. When no one else was her friend, I was. When other kids made fun of her in junior high, I was still her friend. Alexis came from a relatively low income family. There were 6 of them growing up in a cramped two bedroom apartment. Her father worked for 40 years as a janitor. Her mother never worked a day in her life, other than babysitting on occasion for a neighbor or catering a party with homemade food. She had two sisters and three brothers. Her mother and father were among a dying breed. They are still married to this day, despite all of the ups and downs. None of the rest of us in our circle of friends had that, except Camille. Cassie and I didn't. Alayna's mother and father were never married to each other. So anyway, life was hard for Alexis when we were in school. She would take odd jobs after school and all summer long from the time we were 14 to the end of high school. Her oldest sister has been in and out of prison more than the correctional officers and warden. She lives in a cramped one bedroom apartment in Landover, MD. Her younger sister has two sons and a boyfriend who abuses her most of the time. All three of her brothers have done very well for themselves. The oldest brother is a Lead Pharmacist for a large chain drugstore on the East Coast, supervising 2 or 3 locations around the Washington, DC area. The middle brother is a Computer Engineer for the American Prevention of Cancer Society and consults for several major private companies. The youngest brother has a grade 12 job in the Federal Government as a Laboratory Scientist. Whatever ambition was instilled in the boys was lost in translation in the girls. All through school, Alexis was a bit less trendy than the rest of us. When we were getting our little outfits from Marianne's, Lerner's, and Hecht's, she was shopping at Kmart – before Jaclyn Smith was trendy... Her mother wouldn't let her do anything with her hair. While we were sporting our A-Symmetrics and Bob styles, she was wearing a mushroom or ponytail. I still was her friend, because trends didn't matter me then and still don't matter now. When she turned up pregnant in high school by the Mr. Universe that the school "whiz kid", Selena de la Hoya, was in love with and everyone was shunning her for not being in the in crowd and getting pregnant by a guy at the top of the "A" list, I was there. I defended her. When we got older and she fell on hard times, I was always there. I paid her electric bill before I paid my own. I bought her groceries when she had nothing in her cabinet other than ketchup and mustard. I picked her up and took her to the hospital at 2am on a work night because the ambulance would have charged her a fee and sent her a bill she couldn't pay. I could go on for days. Don't get it twisted, she had my back too. When I had no one to keep the kids so that I could do simple things like get my hair done or go to the dentist and Aunt Lena was out of town or my mother wouldn't keep them, she did. What she did for me probably pales in comparison, but she knew I always had her back. We would go on capers together – like Lucy and Ethel. We would go try things together we were apprehensive to try alone, like a new high end restaurant or a new stadium church.

One day, Alexis' daughter Rhianna was given a cat by this boy she was dating. It was actually a kitten that was given away prematurely from its mother. Alexis was upset at Rhianna for bringing the cat home to their new apartment, when she wasn't ready for pets, but she let her keep it. There was just one problem, what to feed it. Alexis got on the phone and called me, knowing I had raised feral kittens in the past and that I would know what to do with it. I went over to her place and brought the kitten home with the understanding of giving it back when it was big enough to eat solid food (about another month). I raised the little cat, named "Beloved", and I asked Alexis when she wanted her back. Alexis said, "Just a little while longer", meaning she wasn't ready for Rhianna to have that responsibility yet. Hey, I was cool with it. The boys had grown attached to her too. Finally, Rhianna called me one day and asked if the cat was ready. I told her yes and to ask her mother if she was ready for it – I wasn't getting in the middle of that one! So she asked Alexis. Alexis then called me and finally caved and I told her I would bring the cat Friday, when I knew they would be home in the evening. I took "Beloved" over there and left her with them and the instructions how to set the sand pan and food up and everything they needed to know.

Everything seemed fine. On Rhianna's birthday, February 1st, I took a cake and some balloons over to her house because I knew Alexis was too broke to do anything for her birthday and I wanted my Godchild to have a special birthday. Rhianna was at the movies with Alexis' younger sister Tamara when I got there. I left the stuff and she called me as soon as she got in to thank me. This young girl that Alexis claims to have been "mentoring" was over her house. I was beginning to wonder who she was, because the last 5 or 6 times she was there like she was family, but something about her just didn't set right with me. We would all find out later on exactly who she really was.

About a week after the birthday, the "Beloved" cat got sick. She had eaten something the apartment complex had put down to kill bugs. Nobody saw the stuff up in the corner of the hall closet but Rhianna figured out what it was, long after the fact. Before Rhianna figured it out, Alexis came home from taking care of her Uncle Henry while her Aunt Vivian was at work. She called me on speaker so that they could both tell me about the cat. I asked Alexis all the pertinent questions, "Did the cat eat something, did it fall, did Rhianna possibly drop her, did one of you step on her?" These were questions that would help assess the situation. Alexis said, "No", and I didn't hear Rhianna. I asked, "Rhianna, are you sure nothing happened, she didn't fall off of something." So then I gave them the number to the 24-hour pet hospital. After I didn't hear back from them, I called, maybe about two hours later. Nobody answered the phone. I called Alexis' cell phone and she did not answer that either. I left it alone for a day or two. When the weekend rolled around, I called again. I still didn't get any answer. I was starting to wonder what was going on, so I left a message this time. When Monday came, I asked Cassie if she had talked to Alexis. She said they had gone to church together Sunday. I asked her if something was going on and she said she didn't know of anything (but she really did). Later in the week I told Cassie about the cat incident. To me it was no big deal. Maybe Alexis was looking for me to come running to get the cat and bail her out like I always did and I wasn't going to do that this time. Maybe she got mad because I asked if they stepped on the cat. I didn't know what it was, but it seemed strange to me. After about two weeks of not hearing from her, I asked Cassie to tell her to call me, since I had established that I was the only one she was ignoring. Cassie told her and she didn't say much, so I left it alone. Two more weeks passed. I called her on a Sunday night. Rhianna answered the phone. She said that Alexis was busy and she would call me back, she told her to say that. I asked Rhianna how she was doing, how school was, if she was ok. She told me about an event she took part in at school and that everything was ok. Nothing seemed off to me about her. I knew Alexis wouldn't be calling me back, so Wednesday I mailed her a letter. I told her I didn't know what I did to offend her, but I would appreciate her telling me what is going on so I could gain some understanding. After 21 years of friendship, there should be nothing we can't say to each other. I also told her she could always pick up the phone when she needed a ride, money, or a shoulder to cry on and this is no different. Three days later, I got this long letter full of garbage about how she had been wanting to distance herself from me for quite some time, that I am nothing but a razor tongued monster who says mean things to people. I hurt her daughter's feelings accusing her of stepping on the cat – the #%$&^%$ cat. Oh ok, so I let that go. I wrote her a letter to get it out of my system, but I didn't mail it. I was sitting there thinking, all the money she got out of me over the years, how when she fell on her job and couldn't work and the disability check ran out and all she had was a can of peas in her pantry and a jar of relish, I brought her groceries. At 2am, I left my own kids alone, to drive 3 miles to take her to the hospital. I paid her electric bill twice before I had even paid my own. When Filbert broke her heart and she had come home to find him butt naked in the bed with her church buddy, I came and got her and kept her for two days so he could get all his stuff out of her place without confrontation. When she was up all night lamenting over her near death accident that we don't talk about much, I was there. All the times Filbert robbed her, took advantage of her, used her, I was there and never once passed judgment. But I am now some razor tongued monster? Now I am a bad person?

In the months that followed, I proceeded with my hunt for a house. I tried three times before I outbid someone on a house and actually won! A few houses I was interested in ended up being yanked off of the market. A few others had investors with an inside advantage muscling in on them. I had the cash, but not more than the investors. The competition was stiff. I didn't realize how aggressive these investors can be, when it comes to competing for prime properties. It was a long time coming, but I persevered and made it happen, and I got a nice dwelling that I was comfortable with. It had been a long while and I hadn't spoken to Alexis in any way, shape or form. I had no reason. She had chosen to put her big butt on her back and act like an ungrateful ingrate. Why would I share good news with her? She would try to turn it around to me bragging about my good fortune or me trying to put he down. I know I wasn't the true optimist when she moved into subsidizec housing. I think where she moved to was the most ghetto place in the area Alayna used to work at the school over on the next block from her. A largr portion of the student population lived in that complex. It was like its owr little self contained village in the hood. The inside of each unit was very nice The buildings were well lit, but the rift raft that resides there makes you wan to not park your car in the lot. I know my words were less than totally supportive when I found out she was moving there, but it was out of concerr for her and Rhianna. Let's be real, she already lost control of Rhianna som time ago, did she think it was a good idea to put her in the midst of a wa zone and expect things to get better? I didn't say much, but I said enough. only went over there maybe 3-4 times. But I knew it wasn't the place wanted to hang out in, friend or no friend. You could hear babies crying, kids yelling, loud stereos blasting, cars pulling up honking, doors slamming, it wa a bit noisy and full of traffic at times. I guess Alexis was just so taken by having more room and being off the waiting list that she just went for it regardless of the surroundings.

LIFE GOES ON

I bought my house and moved into the suburbs of PG County, MD. With new responsibilities, bigger expenses, and all the unpacking I would have to do, I didn't have time to be worrying about Alexis. Cassie was the only person in our group really speaking to her on a regular and consistent basis. It was as though Cassie was trying to monopolize Alexis's friendship. Out of thin air, I received an email in my Yahoo account from Alexis. "Best Wishes", she called it. It was an email that she started out pretending to congratulate me on my home, but then quickly went south with how razor sharp my tongue is, how depressed I've always been – pretty much a segue into telling me how bad of a person I am. She went on to throw my past up in my face. I haven't been that old person in ages, but that is all she could think of to throw out there. She couldn't see all the dinners, the trips to Wal-Mart, the Lucy and Ethel adventures. No, everything I have ever said has been an attack. It's ok, I was growing into being fine without talking to her, without her constant crises, without her draining neediness. I was coming into peace, although I wondered if my god-daughter Rhianna was ok on a daily basis. I even wrote Rhianna a letter about the cat incident, but Alexis took it and turned it into me trying to still accuse her of stepping on the #@$#^$## cat! Alexis was on a crusade to try to turn as many people against me as she could. Unfortunately for her, more people love me than she realizes, so her plan wouldn't work, but she tried anyway. She went to Collette with some nonsense. Collette shut her down like Windows 98! She got mad when she couldn't get anywhere with Collette so she ended the conversation with her signature catch phrase, "I rebuke you in the name of Jesus Christ." Collette was thinking to herself, "WHATEVER", and she let it go. Alexis then went to the one friend she has outside our circle who I never liked and proceeded to paint this dismal picture of me. Then the friend say to her how did she tolerate me all these years? How dare she? She doesn know me like that. If I wasn't the person I am today I would whoop her as But it showed how simple Alexis was thinking at the time. She alway proclaimed herself to be an evangelist, but her actions, at this point, wen more hypocritical than anything else. She always wanted to throw scripture into everything. If you asked her if it is raining, she had to find a scriptur not a yes or no. She had the nerve to want to judge you for whatever sh thought you were doing wrong, but she was the same one who just a wee before moving, bragged to me how she "fucked" Filbert's brains out and sen him on his way – her words, not mine! That's real evangelical! Oh s Christian-like. One Sunday, after church, Alexis Cassie and I were havin brunch at the buffet place down the street from the church, when I decide to get up to go to the ladies room. Cassie was going to go too, but Alex nudged her to stay – so she could talk about me. When I came back, Alex attacked me about this guy I dated for all of 15 minutes. She had the nerve t say to me, "I rebuke you in the name of Jesus Christ", and proceeded to fak like she was speaking in tongues. I never brought up Filbert to throw back a her, I let her give her sermon and cite her scriptures, without a word o rebuttal. Ever since then, it seemed that she and Cassie started doing thing more together, going places, and excluding me intentionally. When this fak email came up, I knew Cassie had to be the one that dropped a dime abou the house. I didn't confront her, but I figured it out. Collette doesn't talk t Alexis much. Alayna and Camille don't talk to her unless we are all in a grou setting. If it looks like a duck and quacks like a duck, it sure isn't a turtle!

After some more time passed, I casually said to Cassie, "You know Alexis sent me an email, pretending to congratulate me on my house. I was bit surprised because I hadn't been talking to her and I hadn't told her abou the house." Cassie got quiet. All of a sudden she remembered something sh forgot to do and scrambled off the phone. A half hour later she calls me bac with an idea to have us talk to a mediator (Alexis and myself). Hmmm Where did that come from? I didn't say much of anything more than "okay' even though to me, my friendship was over with Alexis. She had establishe a pattern of unwarranted and unacceptable behavior. I always forgave and le her back in. Not this time. I took this to my church pastor (when Cassie Alexis, and I went to church together it was Alexis' church usually). He tol me some good things. He said that keeping bad company corrupts mora character (1st Corinthians). He said that you have to ask yourself why you want to fraternize with people who would only bring you down or want to keep you at their level when they aren't rising to the occasion. How can you be friends with someone so easily influenced by another individual? True friends make their own decisions and draw their own conclusions. What is keeping you bound to them? What are you gaining out of the situation? What are they gaining? Is it building character on either part? Does this friendship glorify GOD? That last sentence resonated in my head along with his sermon, "FOOL DON'T BE STUPID". I felt like a fool. One of my last conversations with Alexis was when she was crying about being used by Filbert. She paid his car note, she gave him gas money (when she was working, before a bad accident took her away from her job), and she gave him money to get his insurance straight so he wouldn't lose his license. She felt so used, so stupid. Not once did I put her down for the bad decisions. I did not judge. Well that same way she felt about Filbert was how I felt at that moment about her. I was used. My usefulness had passed and now that she found comfort in Cassie, because Cassie wouldn't say anything she wouldn't want to hear and is very non-confrontational, I was dismissed. Misery loves company, and Cassie seemed to have more than just the daily recommended allowance. In Alexis' method of thinking, I should have been gone from the picture, banished, exiled. I was a cretin. Now that my life was on an upward swing, what good was I anymore? It's funny, because at the same time all of this was happening, I had run into the young lady I saw at Alexis's house during Rhianna's birthday week. She waved to me from the other end of the isle of the store. I waved back, but my 6th sense was starting to nudge me about approaching her. This was the perfect time, so I worked my way down the end of the isle. I asked her how she was doing. She asked me what brought me to the store that day. We had a nice little chit chat for two people who really didn't know each other. I asked her flat out, "Where do you know Alexis from?" She smiled and came back with, "She took me under her wing at the church in the Women's Deliverance Ministry." My next thoughts were of what on earth would she need deliverance from, drugs? Could it have been alcohol? Was it even an addiction? I guess the young lady read it all over my face and she said to me, "I'm not a drug addict or an alcoholic. I don't molest children or knock over liquor stores. I have been asking God to deliver me from being a Lesbian." I guess my next thoughts were, "Why would she want to be delivered from that?", because the way she said it led me to believe she didn't really want deliverance, but was doing it because she

thought that is what everyone wanted her to do. I just said, "Oh", and v
went on to talk about other little chit-chat things before my cell phone ra
and I had to excuse myself.

In the days that followed the different "revelations" I had about t
situation, Alexis felt compelled to send me another email attack, similar to t
first one. A statement in the attack confirmed my suspicions about Cassie
role in all of this. Alexis wrote, "You know I am not the only one you ha
said hurtful things to." Cassie is the only common denominator in th
picture, so from that, I drew the conclusion that Cassie was to be watch
closer than ever and to make sure I dealt with her with the longest handl
spoon I could find. In this email she had the audacity to tell me that I need
ask GOD for more deliverance from all of my imperfections. Like she w
some kind of saint? After talking to that young lady in the store, finding o
she is a Lesbian, and seeing all the time she was spending around Alexis,
started to wonder. I didn't really care enough to give it the time of day, but
found it peculiar that she could judge me and tell me I need deliverance ar
she is sitting in a proverbial glass house with a handful of stones she is rea
to throw. She doesn't even realize that the stones will bounce back at her ar
break her own glass. She's so busy thinking she is better than everyone els
Get a grip!

It's funny how when it rains it pours. I had been sitting there feelir
like the third wheel with one of my own best friends, Camille, and my oth
buddy from the olden days, Jonathan; I had been blind-sided by Alexis in
Mack Truck full of emotions, and then when I figured Cassie into th
equation I just wanted to ask, "Is there room for it to get any worse?" The
the phone rang. It was Camille. I looked at the caller ID and let the phon
ring 3 more times before haphazardly answering, "Hell-Low". I said it, as
my dog had just been hit by a car. "What's up?" She cheerily greeted me. M
smart behind had to answer, "The sun in the sky, what else would be up?
She came back with, "Boy oh boy, what has you down in the dumps?" An
then she hesitated. I think it dawned on her how awkward she and Jonatha
had made me feel. She quickly recanted, "Never mind, I think I know what
bothering you." Before she could say anything else, it just came out, "D
you? Do you really? I have been abandoned and betrayed by two peopl
who I thought were my best friends in the entire world – and no, before yo
ask, you are not even in the equation (I gave her the condensed version of th

Alexis/Cassie scenario)". I also brought up how I really felt when she shared her little romance with Jonathan with me. I really wish she had presented it differently or maybe not at all. I don't know what the purpose was for her to tell me. Maybe she didn't want me to find out some other way, but it sure didn't boost my morale one way or the other. It was just another case of "Miss America and her third runner-up shadow" (I felt lower than second runner up at this point). With that, we got off of the phone. Maybe about an hour later, Camille showed up at my door. I knew she was going to do that, so I purposely didn't go anywhere. I opened the door and noticed that one of the neighbors must have inadvertently received a piece of my mail and they stuck it in the door. It was a card from – of all people – Javier. He was announcing his new 1.2 million dollar home that he and Miss Catrice Simmons had just occupied. Great! I should care, why? Was he doing this to try to make me feel like he's better off without me or was he saying, "This is what you could have had if you were more passive?" or "This is what you could have had if you gave me more access to your resources." I reiterate, "Who cares?" To top everything all off, while Camille and I were sitting at the kitchen table chatting, Erick called. He wanted to know if he could pick the boys up the following weekend instead of having them this week. I didn't have a problem with it, nor did I care to know why, but he had to throw out there that the home wrecker, the BIG little young girl I caught him with at his aunt's house, the same one he secretly married (like no one would find out), had given birth to a boy (BIG FREAKIN' DEAL)... Again, I ask "Do I care? Why?" Is this the season of "Dump a ton of bricks on Mandy while she's down?" Criminy! What's next? Is a house going to land on me or what? I mustered up the nerve to read through Javier's invitation. I don't know why I like to torture myself like that, but evidently, I do. The inside of the card had a postcard with a picture of the front of the house on one side and pictures of the interior on the other. The fine print read when the open house was, the address, and driving directions. I had no intention of going, no idea why he sent me that, and I began to start second guessing myself and my accomplishments in life – big mistake...

THE DAYS THAT FOLLOWED

I began to ponder things in the deep recesses of my soul. How coul Alexis turn on me like such the angry pit-bull she had become? What wa Cassie's problem that she had to go and talk about me behind my back like stole her boyfriend? Lord knows that wasn't the case. I stepped back fror Cassie for a minute. I needed space. During the time I left her alone, I wasn answering her calls. She called me 3 times a day on every number I had, like crazy person! What was that about? Cassie often bragged on how smart sh was. She always prided herself on how many degrees she had, two Associate' two Bachelors, and a Master's. So what? She was so proud of how she raise her little sisters while her mom was out working hard 14 hours every day. S what? It turned out her mother was a racketeer. She felt so blessed to be le that Mafia blood money to share with Collette and her two PEASAN' friends, Alexis and yours truly. So what? The men that came into her li were a mirror of her search for self love. She was in a loveless relationshi with a hustler who pimped women behind her back. She thought he was i "Public Relations." Well he was in "Public Relations", but it was just different kind of "relating to the public". She found out when the U.! Marshals, or the FBI or maybe both, I keep forgetting, I wasn't really payin attention, broke into her house and raided it. They turned her house insid out like a cheap turtleneck sweater from the $10 store. It took her 6 month to get it back in one piece. By then, the guy was halfway across the countr and had been on America's Most Wanted twice before a farmer and his wif in Kansas called the hotline on him, leading to his arrest. She then fell hea over heels with an ex-con who stole everything that wasn't nailed down fror inside of her house. That relationship lasted 6 months, in which time h managed to steal: her two MP3 players, a desktop computer she used for he job, a Blu-ray disc player, a 32" Plasma TV, her grandmother's wedding ring, a priceless painting by some dead artist (that was worth more money than you could shake a stick at), two leather coats, a shelf stereo system, her neighbor's sons' Schwinn and Huffy bikes, and her backup car – a 2002 Toyota Camry that she kept for the times she didn't want to showboat in her Hummer or her Lexus. Well, when he was caught in Kansas, he had a rap sheet that extended from sea to shining sea! She did get the Toyota Camry and her Grandmother's ring back through the recovery of stolen items in his possession at the time of his arrest, but everything else was a total loss – and she still didn't learn. The straw that broke the camel's back was one night when Camille, Alayna, Alexis, and myself had been over to her house for our usual monthly women's book club meeting. This CLOWN was supposed to be gone while we met. Camille had to use the restroom so she went to the upstairs bathroom, since the powder room on the first floor was being renovated. This fool had the nerve to force her back in the bathroom and try to convince her as to why he should be allowed to "hit it" real quick while the rest of us were downstairs preoccupied. He put his hand over her mouth and she was trying to fight him. She kneed him in the nuts and dropped the glass cotton ball canister to the floor – shattering it, and raised enough ruckus for the rest of us to come running. Can you believe Cassie took his side? We all left. None of us spoke to Cassie for several weeks after that. Finally, she called us all up, one by one, and apologized. He tried to rape her youngest sister, Sasha, when she was visiting one weekend. Sasha pressed full charges and he was locked up for a long time, not just for the simple assault, but for previous, unrelated crimes. There were too many to count...

PICK UP THE PIECES

Where do I begin to put myself back together? I decided that th best thing for me to do would be to get away for a few days. I asked Aur Lena to keep the boys and she agreed. I took a long weekend, Thursda through Monday, and flew to Curacao. I made arrangements to stay wit Alayna's Aunt Giselle, who had told me that I was welcomed to stay at hc guest house on her estate anytime I needed to get away. The guest house wa about 100 feet from the edge of the beach. From the side porch, you coul see a perfect view of the sun coming up over the horizon. Aunt Giselle was writer, and somewhat of a mentor to me, from a distance. We would ema each other two or three times a month, during which times she would sen me writing exercises. She even managed to get one of my essays printed i her local paper. I knew this was something I had to do, so I called BW airport and made my flight arrangements. I dropped the kids off with Aur Lena that next night (Wednesday), packed my one bag, and headed to bed s that I could be ready for the shuttle to get me the next morning.

As I rode to the airport on the shuttle, random thoughts began to run through my head:

What is keeping me in the DC area?

Why am I so afraid of relocating and making a new life for myself and the boys?

Could this be the change I needed to take life by the hand and just go with the flow?

What did I stand to lose?

And then it hit me! I have nothing to fear but fear, itself. I called Collette from my cell phone, as I knew she would be the only one up at 5am who wouldn't curse me out for calling so early on a work day. "Hello", she answered. I said to her, "Hey Co, it's me Mandy. I'm on the shuttle for the airport, heading to Curacao today for a 4 day holiday, gotta' clear my head." "I was just thinking about you," she replied. "I had hoped you would take a few days for yourself after all you told me about yesterday. When we talked, you seemed so distraught. You know I would join you if I could, but it is crunch time at work and I am up for the Manager of the Fundraising Department job that opens next week." I went on to tell her, "I've been evaluating some things. When I come back, let's have dinner at Ellis Island Café on Tuesday, if you aren't 'corporately occupied,'" and I giggled. She said Tuesday was a plan, and we hung up. I pulled out my journal and jotted down the pros and cons of relocation. There were very few cons. The shuttle stopped at the airport, I got off and dragged my one bag through to the security gate and boarded the flight without incident. Curacao, here I come!

When the plane landed at the airport, I went and claimed my one bag, headed to the waiting area, and Aunt Giselle came in the double doors and greeted me with a big hug. "Oh my child, you look like you've lost a few pounds, turn sideways." And I did. "Where did you go?" She jokingly teased me. I knew the stress had gotten to me, but I didn't realize how thin I had gotten until we got to her house and I went to change my outfit and my pants were entirely too big. Aunt Giselle laughed at me in those baggy pants, "My, my, my, child. Where did you find those husband repellant clown pants?" W both laughed. She went on to say, "You weren't big as a minute to beg with, now you could almost be Ally McBeal's stunt double. Throw on one o my sundresses and let's go into town." It's ironic that she would say tha Soaking wet in a business suit, Aunt Giselle couldn't weigh more than 100ll her own little petite self! With that, we caught the local bus into town an Aunt Giselle spent about $500 on new clothes for me. She didn't have to d that. It's not like I am broke, I am far from it. I guess she saw that I neede the attention. While we were in town, she took me to the book store, son store with a fruity title, and showed me all of her books on display. Au Giselle had received so many literary awards, so much recognition; I knew that moment that writing was what I was meant to do. We stopped again at small café where we feasted on the best of the best food on the island. As tl sun began to work its way toward setting, we got back on the local bus t head back to her house. It had been a full day. The next day, we got up ear and had breakfast on her veranda. She had a cook who came in and made a three of her meals every day, except the special occasions like our dinner i town. It was exquisite. We talked during breakfast. After breakfast, I put c my swimsuit and headed down to the beach. I sat on the edge of the san letting the waves come just close enough to wet my feet and ankles. Th water was warm and a beautiful clear blue. The waves were gentle as they ju barely lapped over my toes and heels. The sand was soft and conforming t the weight of me sitting in it. It was at that precise moment that it hit me t write a semi-fictional story about my perils in relationships, ordeals with m friends, and dating nightmares we had all survived. I told myself that th perfect title would be "Long Walk off a Short Pier", and with that, I pulle out my journal and began to jot down details for the characters and the stor lines. After about an hour had passed, I moved back from the shoreline an took a shady spot under a beach umbrella. I put the pen and journal dow and began to just meditate in the peace and calm surroundings of the beac As noon approached, I decided to head back to Aunt Giselle's house fc lunch.

Aunt Giselle greeted me at the edge of the walkway, and led me t the deck on the back of her house. The chef had prepared one of my favorit dishes, poached salmon with dill sauce. All of this hospitality and peacefu tranquility almost made me wish I didn't have to go back home. My littl holiday came to a quick closure with Aunt Giselle waving at me as my taxi le her estate. I left her a nice thank you card and a beautiful bouquet in the guest house for all of her generosity and accommodation during my stay. I got back on my flight and headed back home to BWI airport. I called Collette as soon as I landed and she told me she would meet me at the main gate, she was already in the area. She sounded a little concerned, but I wasn't sure if she was just tired or if something else was going on so I just waited until we met up to figure it all out. Collette showed up, just as she said, and my one bag had become two at this point, but I dragged both to the door and she took one for me. I looked at her and asked if everything was ok. She seemed a bit out of sorts. She hesitated with a weak, "Yeah, everything is fine", but I knew her better than that. I put my bag down and hurried up to stand in front of her so she could not pass me. "What gives with you today?" She looked at me and told me she wasn't sure if she should tell me or not. I said, "What?" She just looked at me and put my other bag down. "Okay, Okay", she began to break. "While you were gone these 4 days a lot of things happened. Alexis and Cassie had a big fight over something Rhianna did. Alexis found out that her mother has cancer and has been hiding it from her for about 5 years. Her father confessed to having had an affair for the last 15 years with a school teacher who lived on the next floor down from them. Cassie's youngest sister, the one sexually accosted by the CLOWN, died in a fiery car crash when a drunk driver hopped over the median strip and hit her head on. She had been struggling with some issues and gave up on winning the battle with her demons when the crash happened. That was just a summary of what happened on Saturday. Sunday, I saw Jonathan Daniel and he told me that he is now engaged to Camille. The wedding is set for Next Saturday, not this Saturday because the church wasn't available. Camille is pregnant. Your mother had a nervous breakdown from the doctors giving her the wrong combinations of medications, but she will be okay, and Erick's mother escaped from prison and threatened to kidnap the twins. This was Sunday, rather, yesterday. Today, I got another phone call from Jonathan – actually my husband spoke to him, which was odd, because we didn't really kick it like that with Jonathan and I didn't really know what the conversation was about until just before you called me to meet you. My husband called and told me that Jonathan is having doubts about being with Camille. He said it took him knocking her up and getting engaged to her to see that in reality, he wasn't seeing the forest for the trees." I stopped her. I told her to take a deep breath. I came back with a question, "What did he mean about the forest for the trees, and how could all of this malfeasance take place during my once in a lifetime little 4 day – 3 night vacation? What on Earth Collette just sighed, "Jonathan realized too late in the game that he shou have taken you more seriously. He should have given you mo consideration. Camille's ex-husband has been stalking them, calling her hou and threatening her, showing up at her kids' school, and making life difficu He keyed up Jonathan's brand new S Class." I wasn't too much taken I that. I had a kind of nonchalant attitude about him and her at this point. did ask Collette about the Alexis and Cassie drama and the Alexis and h parents' drama. She told me Cassie had called her about the fight she h; with Alexis. It seemed that they were over Cassie's house and Rhian helped herself to a few of Cassie's belongings without asking. Alex defended her and Rhianna got sassy. Alexis told Rhianna to sit still and I quiet while they fought this out, but she didn't listen. Rhianna confessed having stolen some earrings on one occasion, siphoning thousands of dolla out of Cassie's account over the course of 6 months, and using her identity set up some credit card accounts to go shopping with. Rhianna had becon quite the little "Queen of Set It Off." She stayed in trouble with the la hung out with wild men, among other things. It is unfathomable, the ner of these chicks! Neither Alexis nor Rhianna tried to apologize. Alexis wei totally off on Cassie. After Rhianna had pretty much admitted to stealin Alexis went on to tell Cassie that she needs to look to the Lord for mo; answers and stop being such a promiscuous whore, like her friend Mandy ar the infamous Biblical Jezebel. She threw in some strategic scriptures arour and closed out her thrashing with, "I rebuke you in the name of Jesus Christ Where have we heard that before? She and Rhianna felt that Cassie w; rubbing her good fortune in their faces, versus sharing a genuine blessing. is baffling, considering that Cassie didn't have to give Alexis those thousan(of dollars like she did – blood money or not. And why did she have to ca me names? I wasn't even there. To end it, Cassie yelled back at her, "No is YOU I rebuke in the name of Jesus Christ. I rebuke YOUR OUT O CONTROL DAUGHTER in the name of Jesus Christ! NOW get the H(out of my house!" As for Alexis' parents, Alexis had been over there t check on her mother, since she had just gotten out of the hospital o Thursday. Her mother was crying her eyes out and came out with the affa her father had been having. In doing that, she told Alexis she had termin; cancer and the outlook was bleak. Her father was nowhere to be found. H disappeared for days at a time and the mother never had anything to sa about it.

HMMM...

A week had passed and I hadn't spoken to anyone except Collette, so I decided to give Alayna a call. She was so glad to hear from me. Aunt Giselle had sent her an email telling her about the wonderful time we had when I visited. Alayna seemed a little puzzled so I asked her what was going on. She said that she just had gotten a call before I called her and it was out of the blue from Alexis. With surprise in my voice I said, "What?" She said, "Yes, I know. I don't really deal with her like that, but she called me and I knew she had to be up to something." I went on to question Alexis's intentions. "Well, what did she say to you?" Alayna came back with, "She started by trying to say her church was having an event and she was calling everyone she knew to try to get a good gathering together." The suspicion began to rise in Alayna and she told me that her usual direct self came out at that point in the conversation with, "Ok, what is this really about?" Alexis was transparent, like Scotch tape at this point. She answered with a very condescending, "I just thought this would be a good outing for you and your family to come out and get to know who Christ really is." Now by this point in their conversation, we could all see that Alayna would have been quite agitated by the statements alluding to Alayna not really knowing Christ. Alayna came right back with, "Hold on sister! You don't know me! You don't know what kind of 'mad connections with God' I may already have. I

think you need to get off of my phone now. Thanks, but I don't need yo
judgment." Before Alayna could hang up on her, Alexis blurted out,
rebuke you in the name of Jesus Christ and have a blessed day!" Alay
slammed the phone down. I couldn't believe it, but at least this time s
wasn't bashing me.

By now it was Wednesday, just three days before Camille an
Jonathan were to get married. I went on to tell Alayna that I hadn't seen
spoken to either one of them. Camille had sent me an email asking me to l
her maid of honor, but I never responded. She even said she already had th
dress for me in case I decided to show up at the wedding. I guess she knew
was avoiding her. Alayna told me to stop avoiding them both, because w
had been friends for so long, and to let them know what is on my heart. Sh
felt it would be better that way than to let it all come out in a moment of ra
or fester into something far worse later down the road. What on Earth wou
I say? Would it even matter? Alayna and I had a cup of tea, she showed m
some pictures her kids took when they were with Aunt Giselle a couple
months back, and then I headed home. The boys were with Aunt Lena an
she had told me earlier in the day that Erick's mother had been captured. Sh
was trying to hold up a check cashing place through the bullet proof gla
with nothing more than a plastic knife from Wendy's. Talk about being o
another planet... That was good news. The boys spent another night at h
house and I had some more time to think. When I got home, the phone ran
as soon as I had locked the door. It was Jonathan. He was around th
corner, trying to wait for me to get home and to muster up the nerve to ca
me. I was a bit surprised, as his call caught me way off guard. He asked me
he could come in and I hesitantly told him to come on to the door. He cam
in and I headed back to the kitchen and I mumbled to him to lock the doc
behind himself, so he did. As I heard the lock click, my heart jumped.
dawned on me to ask him if Camille knew he was here. He just looked at m
like a deer in the headlights. He gave me a haphazard "Nope." I turned
loose and didn't go down the road of continuation about that. I asked hir
flat out, "Jonathan, what is this really about?" He looked at me and sai
"Every way you have reacted lately has been well warranted." I looked at hir
with a piercing stare and sarcastically interjected, "I am glad to know I hav
your approval. AS IF!" by this point we were face to face and I was about t
drop a million pieces of pinned up wisdom on him, in other words, give hir
a big piece of my mind, but then out of nowhere, he kissed me. He haule

off and kissed me. Out of reflex, I kissed him back. It was a kiss like nothing I had ever felt before. When I broke free, I was actually dizzy. The room was literally spinning around me and the floor looked as though it was coming up to meet me. I took a few deep breaths. He looked a bit flushed himself. Do you know what he had the nerve to say, once he caught his breath? "I waited too long to do that." I was thinking in my head, "Duh, you dummy! It took you knocking up MY best friend to finally notice me? You are some piece of work!" But I did not say a word out loud. I was still trying to get my pulse back to normal. Just then, he must have sensed me trying to get some words together to throw back at him, so he kissed me again. He backed me up to the kitchen sink and hoisted me up on the counter. Kissing me more passionately than ever, he began to run his hand up my skirt, then up my thigh, and he caressed my backside. I broke free from his breathtaking kisses and asked, "What are you doing?" He smiled at me and said, "I think you know what I am doing." He unzipped his pants, eased my panties off, and proceeded to make the most passionate kitchen counter love to me that any man could ever possibly try to rival. 10 minutes into it, I completely wiped Camille out of my mind, along with her pregnancy, and my status as the 3rd runner up in her perpetual Miss America Pageant. But what were we doing? After a good 20 minute workout, we both had reached our climax and he gently helped me down off the counter. I asked him what we had just done. He just looked at me, gave me a big hug and one more kiss. With that he left. Not another word was said.

Friday morning came; I decided it was time to end my long hiatus from my job, so I called the office to tell them I would be in on Monday. I didn't really need the money, but it was something to do all day until my writing career got off the ground, not to mention the health and life insurance benefits that came along with the job. No sooner than I got off of the phone, it rang. It was Collette. Camille was rushed to the hospital and put in intensive care. I had put her on my "to do" list. I didn't want her going off to get married and the two of us having water under the bridge that hadn't been dealt with properly. I am supposed to be her best friend and I had just slept with her fiancé, the father of her baby. It's ironic. I didn't have much guilt, if any at all, about my encounter with Jonathan. Oh yes, I knew it was wrong on all accounts, but I really enjoyed it. Maybe it was my subconscious feeling of being betrayed by her and Jonathan and now giving back t betrayal. I didn't feel proud either, but I was lacking the guilt I should ha felt. I was wondering, "What's wrong with me?" But then I let it go as hopped in the car to go to the hospital.

MEDICAL

Collette and Alayna were both at the hospital. Although Alayna had only been a distant friend with Camille, when Collette told her what was going on, she asked if she could come for moral support. Collette went and picked her up. Jonathan was on the other side of the waiting room. He was tense. I didn't dare approach him. No one knew what he and I had done the night before, but I didn't want to seem overly eager to express my empathy for whatever he was going through or whatever had happened to Camille. Alayna, being the direct person she is, took the lead and headed over to Jonathan. Flat out she asked him, "What's the deal with ol' girl? What happened to her?" Appreciating her directness, Jonathan got up and called us over to where he and Alayna were. He said that Camille got up early in the morning with severe cramps and bleeding. She called the doctor's emergency line and they thought she was having a miscarriage. When she got to the hospital, the preliminary internal examination did not look good. Camille's cervix was severely compromised. I was becoming anxious. Before I could say anything, Alayna was leading the conversation with, "So what is the bottom line? What does that mean?" Jonathan said to us, "The doctors all seem to think it is cervical cancer." WHOA Nelly! Cervical cancer?! Just then, a doctor came out and asked for her family. We all stood up and Jonathan said, "We are all her family, what's going on?" The doctor was

hemming and hawing and beating around the bush and once again, Alay
rose to the challenge, "Just spill it already." The doctor went on to say th
Camille had stage 3 cervical cancer. They would have to perform a radic
hysterectomy immediately and keep her for a few days for observation
determine if the cancer had spread beyond just her reproductive organs. Th
also meant that the baby that she was 8 weeks pregnant with would also l
aborted in the process. A tear came to Jonathan's eye and we all sat
disbelief. This would have been his first child and now he will never get
know what it is to hold that child or see it off to its first day of school. Aft
a few more minutes passed, another doctor came out to announce that sl
was being prepped for surgery. She had been heavily sedated and surgery w
the only option to save her life. The bleeding would not stop and she risk
bleeding to death if measures were not taken immediately. Jonathan pull
himself together and began asking if this was the universe getting back at hi
for not being loyal to her, for not having pursued me when he had th
chance, and for all the other mistakes he had made along the way. A lac
came into the waiting room. She sat down next to Jonathan. She told hii
she had heard everything from the other side of the door and not to worr
everything happens for a reason. It may not seem like it now, but God has
plan for each and every one of us. Jonathan was numb with grief. He let th
lady talk and in the days that followed, her words came into focus for him.
had loved Jonathan for as long as I had known him. I was sure that aft
Camille pulled through all of this, the wedding would be back on, so I ke
my distance, not just from him, but from her too. We never spoke of th
tawdry night of passionate sex on the counter again…

RESILIENCE

Camille pulled through the surgery fine and recovered. The cancer had not spread beyond her uterus and she was able to resume normal life. Jonathan called me one day out of the blue. I was leery of taking his call, but I did anyway. He wanted to talk to me about life. Things between him and Camille went south really fast. Her ex-husband came up to Jonathan's job and tried to get him fired, but security escorted him out of the building. The ex-husband had violated the restraining order Camille had against him – twice in one week. She was afraid to sleep, go anywhere, let her kids out of her sight, even breathe. Jonathan couldn't stand much more of it and was beginning to drift away from her. In just a couple of months, the relationship had ended. Again, I felt no feelings either way about the situation. I told him I was sorry to hear that, even though I really wasn't, and we got off the phone. Later that evening, Camille called me. She was crying. She was so sorry for how she kept flaunting her love affair with Jonathan in my face. She said it was never her intent to make me feel like the 3rd runner up in her own personal Miss America Pageant. I told her it was ok, not to worry about it and we got off the phone.

FORGING FORWARD

Wanting nothing more than to move forward in my life, I submitte
two manuscripts to my agent for submission to several big printing venue
As I worked my Management Analyst job at DOJ in the daytime, I als
worked on my third project in my spare time. In about two weeks, I got a ca
from my agent saying that a very big publisher was interested in my firs
project and another well known publisher was interested in my secon
project. I was pumped! My agent set up two meetings, one with eac
printing company; one for Friday morning and one for the afternoon.
wasn't very impressed with the bigger publishing house's desire to alter
great deal of my content. I let my agent know that this was not going t
happen. The second meeting, however, turned out to be most productive.
agreed to work with one of their editors; they even decided that they woul
take on my first project as well, and I got a $100,000 cash advance for m
book that same day. The following Monday, I went to work at DOJ an
turned in my 2 week notice for resignation. I contacted my health insuranc
company and bought a two year policy of coverage for the kids and myself.
took a couple of hours that evening to contemplate my next move while th
kids were watching a movie. At the end of my contemplation, I decided t
move to King and Queen County and live on my Virginia Farm. I didn'
need the job anymore; I still had most of Cassie's blood money, the $100,00

advance, and the money I had put aside the past few years. I walked away from a non-supervisory GS-13 job, which is rare (usually by the time you get the GS-13 you have supervised people), to follow my dream. I was looking forward to leaving everything behind; the failed relationships, the betrayal by my so-called friends, and the drama from everything I went through with Javier, Erick, and even Jonathan. I would miss Alayna the most, but I had to go and find inner peace.

I closed out all of my affairs and relocated to the farm on Route 721 in Newtown, VA. The first day there, I decided not to unpack. School had just let out the week before, and although I was concerned about Caleb and Kalen adjusting to being away from their friends, they immediately ran across the cornfield to my cousin Olivia's house and started playing with her younger son in their back yard. After about an hour, I shut my front door and crossed the field to join them. Olivia motioned to me from the yard to join her on the porch where she poured us both a glass of lemonade. She was off for 4 days from her job as the lead baker at a big cookie factory in Richmond. We sat outside as the trees swayed in the breeze. There is no scent sweeter than the country air in King and Queen County, VA. Just before dusk, Olivia's older son started the barbecue grill. He would be going off to Florida A&M University in Tallahassee in August. She would miss him. Ever since her husband died in Iraq in 2004, she has leaned on him to be her support. Now he will be leaving, which further confirms that moving to Newtown was the right decision for me. I would be about a half an hour from Grams and I would be there to support Olivia – actually we would support each other.

As the days turned to weeks, weeks turned to a couple of months. A full year had passed. The first school year in a new county went fine for the twins. Olivia's older son, Troy, had done well for himself during his first year of college. I was thinking back to all I had left behind in the city. Collette was the only one I spoke to on a regular basis. I spoke to Alayna by email once, maybe twice a week. I hadn't spoken to Camille but once since she got out of the hospital. How could I face her? I slept with her fiancé. At times I felt like it was my fault that all of the tragedy that happened that day had happened. In reality, I knew it wasn't my fault; it was just the universal destiny. I still had moments of guilt, but I would suppress them and just move on instead of letting them consume me. I felt that she was wrong, knowing that I always had a thing for Jonathan, to proceed into a relationship but I rationalized that if he wanted me he would have come after me. He went after her – and that was that. I had to come to a point where I no longer lived in her shadow and the only way I knew how to do that was to back away. Looking back, that may not have been the best tactic, but it was the only one I could reach for at the time. I knew eventually I would have to face her again, if for no more than my own ability to let go, but I didn't know how soon it would be.

SAY WHAT?

I was curled up in my oversized recliner when I got a phone call. "Hello?" I was wondering who was calling me at 7am on a Saturday morning way down here on my cell phone. I kept my DC "202" area code number, just because all of my family and those who had always been my friends in the past had it. I didn't see the point in changing it to an 804 number when only a few cousins and Grams were in that area code. At the other end of the line a familiar male voice asked me, "Is this Mandy London?" I was beginning to wonder what was up so I responded, "Who is this?" He answered, "Sorry, this is Lieutenant Grayson with the Police Department (like I didn't remember him)." I interrupted him without personal and social conversation and asked, "Grayson, cut the formalities. What is this about?" He continued, "We have a situation here at the Motel XYZ, in which a young woman was found dead in a hot tub, an apparent suicide." I was stunned. I cut him off. "Why are you calling me about a suicide in DC? I'm two hours away in Virginia!" He said, "Calm down, woman! You were the first name on the list on the page she left open in the room. There are 5 more names I have to call." I doubled back with "Say WHAT? Like who?" Of course, Grayson wasn't supposed to tell me the names, but I think he didn't really care at this point and knew I was upset so he rattled off Camille, Cassie, Alayna, Collette, and Filbert. I asked, "Who was found dead?", because at this point I pretty much figured it was Alexis, only because the name Filbert was on the list, an Alexis's name wasn't. I asked again, "So who is the victim?" He paused minute, while rifling through the wallet on the table, "Alexis..." I dropped the phone before he could say her last name. I balled up in the corner of th living room. Tears began to stream down my face. I woke the boys u grabbed my phone, made sure everyone was dressed. I told the boys to gra something from the kitchen to eat. I called Olivia and told her I would b heading up to DC for a while and asked her to keep an ear out for the hous and asked if she would look after the boys while I went to DC. She agree and I was off. I must have gotten to DC in record time, an hour and a hal The roads were clear and not a state trooper was in sight. I got to the mote where the police had roped off the entire lobby. Guests were asked to sta put until the investigation was finished, in order to avoid disturbing th evidence. I ran inside the lobby doors, through the crowd. I saw Cass standing near the door. I saw Alayna standing by herself near the counter. saw Collette sitting by the elevator talking to Camille. It was weird. We wei all in one space again. Before I could say anything to anyone, the elevator be went "ding" and the doors opened. The coroners were bringing her boc through the lobby on a gurney. She was a big, thick girl, but they shoved he body in a regular vinyl body bag just the same. It took two coroners to pus and one to guide the front to get her through. Just as they approached th door, Cassie, Alayna, Collette, Camille and I rushed over to the coroner The police tried to hold us back, but Cassie bum rushed her way past the tw average sized officers to grab the zipper and in a split second, rip it ope enough to expose Alexis down to her shoulders. We all screamed out. Cassi hit the floor. Camille began to cry out loud. I was totally numb. Alayna wa even sobbing and she wasn't nearly as close to her as the rest of us had beer Slowly but surely, Collette and Alayna began to scrape Cassie up off of th floor. When I saw that her legs were like spaghetti, I stepped in to lend hand. We all got her up on her feet and ended up in a somewhat of a grou hug. We were all crying, together. Cassie was apologizing at being s difficult. She apologized to me for seeming like she was siding with Alexis i putting me down and pushing me away. Collette was apologizing for bein so emotionally unavailable and self-absorbed with her new marriage. Alayn was comforting us. I apologized to Camille for shutting her out of my lif completely. No man is ever worth that. When the men leave you in th dusty ashes of your former self, your friends are all you have left to fall bac on. We stayed there for a moment as they loaded her into the back of th coroner's truck. Lieutenant Grayson, who had called me on my cell phone, came over to us and asked if we wanted to go up to the room. Cassie was apprehensive, but she finally nodded yes with the rest of us. We took the stairs. When we got to the 3rd floor, it was the 2nd room on the right. An officer in the hallway opened the door. We went in and saw her day planner, still sitting on the table. None of us had the nerve to touch it, so Alayna – the fearless leader – took the page in her hand and flipped it from our phone numbers. The next page had a long note written on it that spanned 3 more pages. I just remember the main points and the overall message in it.

Dear Friends,

It is with great sadness that you are probably finding this lette Please know that I never meant to hurt all or any of you that hav found me this way. I never wanted to admit to my own sho comings. I lost control of my daughter long ago. I lost control of m own life and hid behind the bible. I am the ultimate in hypocrisy. threw scriptures at each of you in an attempt to deny my ow skeletons in the closet. I rebuked you all in the name of Jesus Chris pretending that my Christianity was a license to judge everyone els while ignoring my true self in the process. That young lady I wa supposed to be counseling, supposedly helping find her deliveranc from homosexuality, well, she was my biggest secret. We had bee seeing each other for quite some time. She told me two weeks ag that she had AIDS. We had parted ways a year ago. She called me u because she was back in town. We had lunch and she told me. I g tested that next day. A few days later, the doctor called me into th office and I found out that I had it too. I couldn't keep up the charac any longer. I can't save souls and help others get delivered if I was spiritual mess myself. I would host "swinging" parties in hotel room and even pimped a few other church members for money, using th Lord's desire for us to have the treasures of our hearts as the excus I'm so sorry that it had to come to this. I guess you could say that had to take my "Long Walk off a Short Pier". Please forgive me. love you all; despite everything I said or did to each of you. Pleas take care of my daughter for me.

Peace Out,

Alexis

With Alexis' successful suicide attempt and her own letter referencing taking a "Long Walk off a Short Pier," I felt it was confirmation from the Universe to keep that as the title for my impending book. In the weeks to come, I was in and out of meetings with my publisher, traveling for book signings and promotions, and going back and forth from the farm in VA to engagements all over the East Coast. I ran into a small snafu. I needed to boost my publicity. The publishing house was doing a fair job of promoting my books, but I still felt that there was an untapped market. I had struggled with finding a marketing firm that would do me right. After sifting through what seemed like dozens of companies, one kept coming to the surface. JD Marketing. After the 3rd time seeing the firm listed in my research, I went ahead and called to set up an appointment. They were based in Washington, DC. The confirmation was given to me for a meeting that following Monday at 9am. When I arrived at the firm's headquarters on K Street in NW, I kept saying that this building looked familiar. I couldn't place it. I had the strongest sense of Déjà vu that I had ever had in my life. I pressed the elevator button and went up to the 4th floor. A big sign with silver embossed letters "JD Marketing" hung over the door. I went in the double doors and headed straight to the receptionist. I stated, "Mandy London here for the 9am meeting." I was about 10 minutes early. The receptionist buzzed someone in the back and a muffled voice said, "Send her back to the conference room." The receptionist pointed me to the conference room and I headed down the hall. When I got to the end of the hall, I opened the heavy wooden door and peeped in cautiously. There was a lady on the right side of the table and a man on the left. They asked if I was Mandy London. I nodded yes. The lady told me to come on in and help myself to some coffee or tea and snacks. I grabbed a half of a bagel and a small pack of cream cheese and poured myself some coffee. I sat next to her at the table. She said to me, "Our CEO heard about your books and insisted on preparing the package for you himself. Here are some reading materials for you to look over. My associate and I will leave you to read them. If you have any questions after your meeting, here is my card", and she handed me her business card as they both walked out the side door. I finished my bagel and half of the cup of coffee when I heard a knock at the door. I said in a hesitant tone, "Come In." Guess who it was! Jonathan Daniel. I looked like I had seen a ghost. What on Earth would I say after all that I had been through with him going after my friend Camille? Her relationship with him kind of altered my relationship with her. I had to sit and watch them prepare to get married, knowing that it should have been me. I finally had conquered the guilt of the "kitchen counter sex" and feeling like everything that we wrong with him and Camille was because of my momentary indiscretion wi him – and here he comes! Was I up for reopening a door that I felt shou have never been closed in the first place? 10 seconds into my rationale in r head all I could hear is "YES!!!" And with that, I proceeded to complete t paperwork and retain him as my advertising entity.

In the weeks to come, Jonathan Daniel, or JD as he was no referring to himself, and I spent a lot of time together. We had dinner eve night that I was in town. He would drive down to King and Queen Coun to stay with me on his days off. When I went on tour, he came out 10 tim in 6 months to be by my side. I hadn't had much to say to Camille, or tl other ladies for that matter. Collette would send me an email every wee and we spoke that way, but it wasn't the same after Alexis killed herself. V all found ourselves reassessing the meaning of life. As the weeks turned in months and my two books climbed the New York Times Bestsellers List rank in at number one and number two for 12 weeks straight, I four Jonathan to be getting even more serious about me. Camille called me or day, then Alayna right behind her. Collette was the last one to call me and had to break her down to ask what was up. It seemed that Rhianna had bee bounced around from foster home to foster home to foster home to fost home. She was being abused. None of them wanted to tell me what w going on because they knew that at one point, Rhianna meant as much to n as my own kids, but I had eventually backed off from anything that w associated with Alexis. After she handed me her big butt on a plate to kiss, pretty much removed her from my priorities. There was no way I would tu my back on Rhianna. Despite her mother's asinine antics, I couldn't leave h out there. Alexis's parents were not up to keeping her. The other sibling had too much going on in their own lives to take on Rhianna. With litt deliberation, I called the child protective services to begin proceedings adopt Rhianna. The girl was going to be 16 this year and I knew she wou be a challenge, with her previous bouts with the law, but somehow, I knew could make a difference where no one else had been able to, not even Alexi I wasn't sure if Jonathan would be cool with it, but when I mentioned it t him, his response was, "That's not even a question, Rhianna is family. W have to take her in." He said "WE", not "you", "WE". I knew then that was on the right path and that he was the man I wanted to spend the rest c my life with. I had never felt so connected with anyone in my entire life. Suddenly, I felt free. I felt like Erick never existed to me and furthermore I was asking myself why I wasted my time with Javier – Javier – Javier, and I couldn't even remember his last name for a split second. Jonathan Daniel finally realized that with me was where he always belonged, that he had been fighting the universe for half of our lives, and that this time he wasn't going to let anything distract him. No more Camille characters, no more distractions, nobody would take his eyes off of me. For the first time in my entire life, I felt like the true prize that I really am.

WARM THAT HOUSE

Alayna had been calling me a lot recently. She was really excite
She was about to buy her first home. She had been renting forever. Wi
both of her kids now in college on scholarships and doing well, she decided
was time for her to step out on faith and do something she always wanted ¹
do. She sent me an invitation to her housewarming party on the thi
Saturday in May, the week after Mother's Day. I was elated for her. I call¢
Jonathan on his cell to tell him the good news and he said, "That's what's u₁
Tell me what time and I'm there with you." I was a little bit apprehensiⱽ
about going, because I got to thinking about Camille. She might show u₁
Was I ready to face her? It's sad that she lost the baby and had all the heal₮
crises, but I was ready to stop avoiding her and deal with everything head o₁
If I was going to marry Jonathan at some point, she would hear about it.
just didn't want her to resent me, even though I resented her for knowir
how I felt about Jonathan and still getting involved with him. I was also
little bit skeptical, because for the past few months I had been planning t₮
wedding of the century without so much as an ounce of support from the₴
women who I thought had been my best friends for the better part of my lif
and I knew they would all probably be there, especially Cassie. It seemed th₴
when my life really started picking up, Cassie was always trying to outdo m
I moved to the farm and got the house going the way I wanted it. She boug₮

a 3.2 million dollar property in Bethesda, MD and later lost it by not keeping up with the payments. She dwindled away all of her mother's blood money on men, gambling and poor spending habits. When I got my Infinity M35, she went and bought the M45 two months later, only to let another one of her sorry men succeed at totaling it for her. I knew I didn't want to deal with her clouds of negativity, but if Alayna invited her, I would just maintain face for her sake.

Alayna's housewarming was a busy event. It was like one big jamboree. She bought a really nice Cape Cod in the Takoma section of Washington, DC. It was a steal of a deal at a time when properties in that area were going for a half of a million dollars or more. Her aunt Giselle had an old coworker looking to relocate and he sold her the property for a little bit over $200,000. People were all over the back yard, which was quite ample. Kids were playing badminton and kicking a ball back and forth. Alayna's uncle Kenneth was working the barbecue grill. The whole block smelled inviting. The neighbors were there. I saw Collette. It is always good to see her. She came over to speak to me. Her husband waved, he was talking to Uncle Kenneth by the grill. Everyone was having a good time, and then Cassie showed up. She came in, barely spoke to anyone. Alayna cornered her by the gate. She whispered in her ear, "I didn't think you would show." Cassie just looked at her and gave a half baked smile. Alayna went on to whisper to her, "If you bring any drama to my happy event today, I'm going to beat you like one of your old boyfriends– MYSELF!" Alayna walked away with a less than easy feeling in her gut. She walked over to Collette and told her, "That child is nothing but trouble. Something is about to brew". At this point in the game, Cassie had hit rock bottom. She was on the ocean floor with the Titanic. She felt she had nothing to lose. All of her money was gone. The men had taken all of her material possessions and whatever dignity she had left, she was just floating about life aimlessly. Reduced to working a 9-5 as a file clerk, she was still able to keep a 1-bedroom apartment in Hyattsville, MD. She drove a 1987 Honda Accord. She cut all of her hair off and wore basic clothes. She was never a beauty queen to begin with, but she really gave up trying to look presentable. Most of us had cut her back to almost no contact. Alayna only invited her out of pity. I walked over to Jonathan and he gave me a hug and we were talking to Collette and her husband when we heard a car door slam from the alley behind the house. Cassie was standing by the back gate when this guy dashed up to the fence

and banged her in the head with his fist. She stumbled. As she stood ba[
up, she reached in her purse and pulled out a Glock 40. The guy broke a[
ran. She gave chase. All you could hear was 5 gunshots. "Pop, pop, po[
pop, pop." Alayna was fuming. She had just told Cassie not to "start [
mess". Nobody went up the alley to check out what happened. Alayn[
mother called the police when she saw the car pull up in the alle[
Surprisingly, they showed up relatively fast. The party continued, believe it [
not. Despite the drama, everyone still had a really good time. Jonath[
shared the good news of our engagement with everyone. Folks played car[
and horseshoes. The food was delicious. Camille never did show up, but th[
was to be expected. It was hard for her at times to face Jonathan after all th[
had been through. I was sure that she would come around eventually.

After a couple of hours passed, Cassie was a distant memory. [
people started leaving the party, Collette and I helped pick up the food ar[
clear out the kitchen. Cassie had been a good friend to all of us at one poin[
but when she went south, she really went south. There was nothing we cou[
do but pray for her. Alayna's mother came over from the kitchen table an[
took us by the hand and led us in prayer. Just then, Collette's husband an[
Jonathan walked in and joined the prayer circle. Alayna's mother asked Go[
to have mercy on Cassie's soul. She also said a special prayer for Jonatha[
and me to have continued blessings during our marriage and the same f[
Collette and her husband. Her last prayer was one for Camille to find h[
way back to her family, meaning the circle of friends that we had been to eac[
other for so long. Alayna's mother is an Evangelist. She's seen things beyon[
speaking. When we left, I felt truly blessed. I gathered the twins and we a[
headed over Aunt Lena's where we would stay until we went back home t[
the farm.

THE NUPTUALS

Jonathan and I had set a date. We were determined to get married later in the year and we chose Saturday, October 27, 2007. The wedding almost didn't happen because Jonathan's father had gotten ill and it was looking like he was going to have to give up his life to take care of him. The doctors said that he had a massive stroke. It was anticipated that there would be a need for constant care. Everyone knew that Jonathan was the best candidate available in the family so it was looking as though he would have become the top choice to care for the father. No sooner than his father spent a few weeks in the hospital, he died from a massive heart attack. Jonathan took it hard. I almost lost him in his grief, but through prayer and much sacrifice, we endured.

Our wedding was to be the wedding to rival all weddings. Kathryn Beaujoulais was the planner. She is internationally known for her elegant and tasteful wedding plans. I had an elegant Donna Karan dress. We had been going to counseling from the week that Jonathan proposed. The mistake most couples make is planning for the wedding and not for the marriage. We were definitely ready. The flowers were ordered. The dresses had been tailored for the last time for the wedding party, and the groomsmen all had their tuxedos. Jonathan and I decided not to go far away for a long and expensive honeymoon. Instead, we would spend a 3 day weekend at h sister's bed and breakfast near Skyline Drive in Virginia and another 4 da family weekend in Florida in the Spring with the twins and Rhianna. I on had one thing troubling me, Camille. Nobody had really heard from her. figured it was time to do something about that. I didn't want to get marrie without my best friend. Notice I didn't say I wouldn't get married withou her... Anyway, I was becoming concerned. It had been some month Alayna had not spoken to her. Collette had not seen hide or hair of he Cassie surely hadn't, she was too busy ducking and dodging and bobbing an weaving the blows of the men in her life. Now that she had been featured o America's Most Wanted, I was certain no one would hear from her. I decide to make a trip to Camille's mother's house in Waldorf, Maryland. Jonatha was off from the marketing firm for a brief respite. He stayed at home on th farm with the boys and Rhianna. I took a little overnight trip to see Mr Althea (that's what we all called Camille's mom).

I arrived at the split foyer brick house that Camille and her brothe grew up in. Mrs. Althea was peeking out the front window and threw ope the front door when she saw me. She came running out the house an hugged me in the driveway. She said, "Mandalay Bay! It's so good to se you!" That's what she and Mr. Althea (Camille's dad) always called me. W walked in the house and up the few steps to the kitchen on the immediat right. I sat in a high stool on one side of the counter, as Mrs. Althea poure us each a cup of coffee. She said to me, "So, how you been, Darlin'? I hea you are getting married." I felt a knot in my stomach. I felt weird. She kne about Camille's fling with Jonathan. What kind of friend do I look lik marrying her dead baby's daddy? Mrs. Althea never once gave me a guilt tri She let me do that to myself. I said to her, "Mrs. Althea, I felt so bad. mean I've loved Jonathan all my life. We always had a silent chemistry, bu suddenly one day, Camille came into the equation. I don't know how you daughter does it, but she has this command for attention. It is like me cannot ignore her. When we are together, I cease to exist in her shadow Jonathan went after her, he didn't go after me, and here he is getting ready t marry me and I know that he had been with her." Mrs. Althea looked at m and said, "Everyone played a role." I looked at her, thinking to myse. "WHAT?" She saw the confusion on my face and repeated, "Everyon played a role." I was expecting her to defend her daughter. I was expectin her to attack me and tell me how bad of a friend I had been. She turned t me and said, "Camille knew how you felt about that man." I looked at her and said, "Yes". She continued, "But did that stop her from proceeding with getting involved with him?" I said, "No". She went on, "And you knew you always had feelings for this man, feelings deeper than the Atlantic Ocean didn't you?" I said, "Yes". And she said to me, "But you never acted on it did you? He never acted on it either did he?" I looked down and replied, "No." She went on to say, "Was it an assumption that he felt the same way? You know what happens when you assume – you make an ASS out of U and Me." I felt a little dumb and I guess she could see it. She looked at me, "Don't feel dumb. You felt it, he felt it. Neither of you did anything about it and Camille just happened to interrupt 'what could have been'. If you think about it, did she really interrupt anything? You are the one that is about to get married to him. Had you acted on your chemistry with Jonathan, my daughter would be dead right now. If she had never gotten involved with him and gotten pregnant, she never would have found the cervical cancer and it could have spread all over her body and taken her life. So don't look at yourself as being less than the friend you have been to her. If anything, you have been the best friend she could have ever had. This is one time that procrastination saved someone's life. Your procrastination with approaching Jonathan allowed the discovery of my daughter's cancer. It sounds crazy, but sometimes good things come from painful and awkward situations." All I could do was sigh.

Camille's dad came in the front door with his keys jingling in his hand. I'm thinking in my head, "Mr. Althea", but I didn't say that out loud. He came in the door and up to the kitchen where he gave me a hug. I said, "Hi Dad" and he laughed, "Oh Mandalay Bay, long-time no see! What brings you here?" and before I could say a word he said, "Never mind, never mind. I know, and I'll leave you 2 to your girl talk." When he left the area I said to Mrs. Althea, "Ok, so where is Camille and does she hate me or what? None of us have heard from her." Mrs. Althea just looked at me. She said, "Why would she hate you?" I said, "Hello, I am marrying her dead baby's daddy. She knew I always loved him and it looks like I am capitalizing off of her misfortune with him." She just looked at me like I was retarded. She said, "I see why you are such good friends, you are just like her. Take off your helmet, stop licking the window, and park the short yellow bus for a minute. Did you hear anything I just said?" I hesitated, "Yes, I heard you say I saved her life by not getting involved with Jonathan, but I got involved with him after her crisis, after her attempt with him fell apart. What on Earth kind of friend does that?" She looked at me again. She picked up the phone. I was wondering who she was calling. She pretended to dial, but didn't really and she said, "Hello, interpreter services? I need a translator over here right away. I have someone real special in my kitchen who is just not comprehending regular English." She hung up the phone and we both laughed. She said to me, "GIRL, if you don't get a grip on yourself." I started to panic, I said "Oh God help me. She had cervical cancer. Cervical cancer is caused by HPV. OH God, I could get it, that could be God's wrath for following behind her and taking up with her dead baby's daddy." She took a glass out of the cabinet and filled it with cold water from the tap in the refrigerator door. I was afraid she was going to throw it at me to bring me back to reality. She put it on the counter in front of me and said, "Here, drink this and take *chill pill*." With that I calmed down. Mrs. Althea said to me, "YOU HAVE been going to the doctor for your regular Pap Smears, unlike my daughter, haven't you?" I said, "Yes". She said, "Ok and have your results been normal?" I said, "Yes". She said, "Did you have a test for HPV? Again, I said, "Yes". She said, "What are you worried about? A bus could drive through your front door and hit you in your own living room, but do you worry about that every day? Cancer runs in our family. There is a serious predisposition for it. I had a full hysterectomy when I was 25 because I kept having abnormal cells. I had just had Camille's brother. The doctors feared that I would develop cancer so they took all of my plumbing. I wanted to have more kids, but living for the ones I had was more important so I had the surgery. Don't worry about that. God is a forgiving God. Don't look for him to punish you, enjoy what you have in life." She took a sip of her coffee and continued. "As for Camille, she is doing what she always has done when she feels guilty, run and hide." I was sitting there wondering what on Earth she has to feel guilty about. I left it alone. Ms. Althea said, "Make yourself comfortable, dinner is at 5 and I am expecting some company." With that took the last sip of coffee, put the mug in the dishwasher to be washed and put my shoes in the hall closet and joined her downstairs in the family room.

DINNER IS SERVED

Evening approached and at about 4:50pm I helped Mrs. Althea put the dinner out on the table. Mr. Althea had left to go help his brother-in-law move some things around in the yard before the weather got cold, in other words he was giving us time to be alone, because he evidently knew more about this evening than I did.

Five o'clock rolled around. The table was set. The food smelled delightful. I was starting to be curious about the company Mrs. Althea mentioned. Somehow, I didn't feel that anything would be a surprise to me. I didn't bank on it being Jonathan. I left him home with the kids. I figured it would be Camille. The doorbell rang. My heart jumped up in my throat. It was Jonathan. I was surprised. He gave Mrs. Althea a hug and came in the door. I looked at him. He said to me, "Before you ask, your cousin is over at the house with the kids." Does this man know me or what? I felt a little relieved, but not more than 5 minutes later, the doorbell rang again. It was Camille. She was at the door when Mrs. Althea opened it. She took two steps in, saw Jonathan, peeped around the corner, saw me, and turned around to go back out the door. Mrs. Althea grabbed her arm and said, "Oh no you don't. You're not running away this time. It is time to face reality once and for all." She dragged Camille back in the house, talk about awkward situations. Mrs. Althea began serving plates. Camille said she didn't feel like

eating, but that didn't stop her from piling up a plate for her just the sam
After all the plates were served, Mrs. Althea said grace. Camille picked at h
plate, as usual. Jonathan and I ate. The food was delicious as always. Camil
didn't have 3 words to say all through dinner, But Mrs. Althea broke th
silence. She turned to Camille, "Ok girl, what is your problem?" Camil
looked baffled and came back with, "Is that what this is, everyone attac
Camille day?" Mrs. Althea cut that short, "You know no one has heard fro
you for weeks, some for months. I haven't seen you in so long that I a
surprised you showed up tonight. What is going on with you? Now is tl
time to get it all out in the air." Jonathan and I sat silent. I was mortified th
she would turn to me next. What would I say? Camille took a sip of wat
and said, "Do you really want to know what is wrong with me? Do yc
really? How would you feel to watch your best friend in the entire world ru
off into the sunset with the man you were going to marry? How would yc
feel to know that you've been gutted like a fish and can never have any mo
kids in life?" Mrs. Althea cut her off again, "Hold on Miss Missy! You sa
you can't have any more kids and that is an issue? What about the 3 girls yc
had with that sorry ass husband you had for all of 15 minutes? You don
even have them! You have the nerve to formulate your mouth to say that yc
can't have any more kids, like that is a problem! Do you forget that I to
have been gutted like a fish, as you call it? Sometimes the life you ca
continue to live is more important than the life you may or may not live if yc
don't take immediate action!" Uh oh, the fur was about to fly. That was
sensitive subject for her, but true nonetheless. Mrs. Althea had been keepir
the kids since Camille had the cancer surgery. Camille would come and g
but the kids stayed. I wondered where they were that night, but Mrs. Alth
already put it out there that her sister had come to take them to her house f
the weekend so that the cousins could all play together. Camille got silen
Mrs. Althea continued on, "Think about it, if you hadn't gotten pregnant th
last time, you could be dead right now. You hadn't been going to the doct
like you should. You have been hiding out who knows where. You bare
talk to me or your father. If you had not had that episode and gone to th
hospital, you might be DEAD – do you hear me? DEAD!!! Did you eve
stop to think what role you may have played in all of this? You pretend tha
you don't know what you look like, but really, I think you let your physic
beauty go to your head. Yes you are attractive, yes you have a body wome
go and get plastic surgery to emulate, you have plenty of junk in the trunk an
the front, but sometimes you lose sight of your common sense in that. Yo

knew that these two people had a silent chemistry. You knew that. Yet he paid you a little bit of attention and you totally ran with it and forced your way into someplace you didn't belong." Mrs. Althea turned to Jonathan and said, "YOU didn't realize what was right in your face all along. Mandy is one of the most beautiful women I know. She doesn't have a 38DD rack and 'Hips Ahoy', but she doesn't have to. She's been right under your nose for a lifetime, but you fell into the same thing that all the other men fall into. It's like the old fable about the dog seeing his reflection in the river. He has a bone in his mouth and he sees the reflection of a bigger bone in the water so he lets the one in his mouth go and ends up with nothing at all for chasing a bigger bone that turned out to not be what it appeared. Do you get where I am going with this?" I was sitting there thinking to myself the only bone in the equation was the one he got every time he was around Camille, like all the other men. I didn't say a word. Jonathan just looked blank, because he knew Mrs. Althea was telling the honest truth. He had to feel like a serious heel. Mrs. Althea turned to me and said, "Why didn't you ever let this man know how you felt? Why do you insist on waiting for the men to come to you? Honey, don't wait for the ship to come in – SWIM OUT TO IT! Get some confidence about yourself!!! You are beautiful inside and out. You have a nice figure, a wonderful disposition, you're smart and humorous. If this man here couldn't see that the last 20 years then maybe he needed glasses or contacts or something. You are more than "Hips Ahoy". It's whatever it is that makes you - you, that kept Jonathan around all these years. Heck, he was probably too intimidated to step to you, as self-sufficient as you are, but he's here now." She turned to Camille and asked her, "So how long are you going to hold this grudge against yourself?" Camille said, "Grudge against myself? She ran off with the man I was going to marry." Mrs. Althea cut her off, "After it was over between you. AFTER! It wasn't working was it?" Camille came back with, "That was beside the point." Mrs. Althea looked at her, "Beside the point how? You can't stop destiny. These two people were meant to be together. You need to learn to watch for signs a little better than you do. You didn't learn anything from your relationship with Larry. All of the signs were there before you married him, but you married him anyway. He wouldn't work, when he got a job – he wouldn't keep it, he made unwise money choices that caused you to have to work harder to make up for it. You kept hoping for him to turn into some kind of prince when he never had it in him to do more or be more than he already was. You've had other guys that you've dealt with that had virtually nothing going for them and you still invested time and interest and who knows what else in them. Along can Jonathan. He had something going for him, but he's a man. You have a b butt. Most men are going to have a hard time ignoring that. Just because man flirts doesn't mean you have to feed into it and get all caught up in it, b you do and you get hurt every time. You saw him as a very 'together' ma the type you always wanted to be with, but weren't really ready for and yc found yourself somewhere you didn't belong. You strained your relationsh with your best friend. This whole thing strained her lifelong friendship wi him and ultimately everyone has been walking around on eggshells. The was enough drama between the fat girl killing herself and the drama with tl other child and America's Most Wanted. Try to limit the drama in your life Everyone was quiet. Mrs. Althea asked, "Where do we go from here? Do everyone leave after dessert and continue the way you've been or will Man have her best friend at her side to usher in the next phase of her life Camille began to tear up. My eyes welled up as well. Jonathan was holding in, but we knew he was crying on the inside. Camille began to cry out, "I' sorry, I'm sorry, I never meant to hurt my best friend." I was sobbing, "I' sorry too, sorry you have such a big ass that commands the attention of a the men in the room." And we laughed through our tears. Mrs. Alth looked over at Jonathan. He stood up, "I'm sorry to everyone in this roo for all the bedlam I have caused. Mrs. Althea, I am sorry I hurt yor daughter. Camille, I'm sorry about how things turned out, but you knew w wouldn't have worked out. Mandy, I am the sorriest to you for not seeir that you were a diamond and always treating you like the old standby. You' not Cubic Zirconium at all." I wanted to giggle but I ran to him and hugge him. He motioned to Camille and she came over for a hug as well. We we hugging and crying and it was a beautiful thing. I said, "I just want my be friend back." Camille said, "You got her." With that, Mrs. Althea broug the cake and coffee out of the kitchen and we all pulled ourselves togeth and enjoyed dessert.

WANTED!

In the days that followed, Camille and I talked every day. She came down to the farm and stayed one weekend and got her dress tailored for the wedding. At this point, my bridesmaids were going to be my cousin Olivia and my good friend Alayna. Camille would be the Maid of Honor and Collette would be the Matron of Honor. Jonathan had Collette's husband and another friend as the Groomsmen. His fraternity brother from college and his younger brother were the two Best Men. Things had smoothed over between Camille and me. I remember we were watching TV on Saturday night when she came to the farm to visit. She brought her daughters and they were playing video games with my sons over at Olivia's house. Olivia's son had designed some cool video games in college and they were enjoying them. For the first time in a long time, as Camille and I were watching TV, I had one of my visions. I saw Camille at a wedding, but it was not mine. She had a very big diamond ring on her hand and the light kept catching it. It looked as though she was on the deck of a boat of some sort. A man steps into the picture, but he is obscure, I can only make out his silhouette as he walks up and hugs her from behind by the railing on the deck, then the vision fades. A minute or two later I had two shorter flashes of her and the obscure man standing at the altar holding hands, facing each other. She was wearing a wedding dress. What was that about? In a few moments of taking deep breaths, I returned to reality. Anyway, we were watching FOX, mo specifically "America's Most Wanted". It seems that old Cassie had bee caught. She was renting a room from an elderly woman in Little Roc Arkansas. The woman's granddaughter had suspicions about Cassie from d one. When the granddaughter's boyfriend came to dinner with her and tl family, Cassie acted nervous and agitated. After they left, they went on tl AMW website and saw her profile. The police came and caught her ju before midnight that night. Oh well, game over. Cassie was caught.

Camille went home on Sunday. I went with her. We went by h parents' house. Where they live in Waldorf, MD is right off of Route 301, c the way to Camille's house. When we pulled in the driveway, her cousin Je and her boyfriend Wes were getting out of the car in the driveway. Jess ra up to Camille and gave her a hug and then she hugged me. Wes gave us bot hugs too. Jess seemed a little bit more excited than usual. I was wonderir what that was about. She said she had a big announcement. I was thinkir that maybe she was pregnant or something. She and Wes had been togeth for some years and they already had a son together. Jess had finishe academy training and was already a US Marshall. Wes had been a PG Coun police Sergeant in Maryland for 8 years and just moved up to Lieutenant la year. They were a real life Mr. and Mrs. Smith, like the Angelina and Bra movie. What else could it be? Jess looked like she couldn't hold it in, but w all went inside and sat in the family room. Jess was smiling from ear to ea She grabbed Wes by the hand and blurted out, "We're getting married!" Sl held out her left hand to show the most gorgeous Marquis Cut diamond rir you could feast your eyes on. "Marriage", I never would have thought of th one. They had been together for so long; it was like they were marrie anyway. Well that's good news. Wes went on to throw in how they will b getting married that following June and have secured a group rate on a cruis line. One thing about Camille's family, they supported each other come He or High Water and would go to any length to support each other.

.

I DO

October 27, 2007 had rapidly approached. The night before the wedding, we had our rehearsal at 5pm. I was going to have the wedding down in King and Queen County at New Mount Olive Baptist Church in Newtown, but I decided that since all of my friends and family were still in the DC Metro Area that we would get married at Jonathan's church, Ebenezer AME in Fort Washington. That is where we got our marriage counseling, so why not? Olivia was my stand in. You know there is an old superstition that it is bad luck for the bride to walk down the aisle for her own rehearsal. After all I had been through, even though I am not superstitious, I didn't want to risk it. The pastor walked us through the ceremony. I had run into an old friend from high school in the grocery store when I was visiting Aunt Lena about a month ago. Her name is Tara Kellye and she sang back-up for Patti Labelle, Mariah Carey, Regina Belle and the late great Luther Vandross. She was with a group in the mid 90's that called themselves "Sandy", because the three of them were light skinned, they all had freckles and sandy colored hair. They actually looked like sisters, even though they weren't related. After Sandy came apart, she released one solo album that went Gold, with two singles that stayed on the Billboard R&B list for 6 and 13 weeks respectively. After that, she went on Broadway for a while, but when the grandmother who raised her died from cancer, she took a break from show business and hasn't been doing much more than a littl songwriting and producing here and there. When we were in high schoo Tara could bring the crowd to tears with her rendition of Jennifer Holiday "I Am Telling You". When one of our classmates was killed in a car accident she sang "His Eye is on the Sparrow" at the funeral and there wasn't a dry e in the house. The original singer I had in mind, backed out on me. She ha some kind of family emergency and had to fly to NY. I presented th opportunity to Tara and she jumped at it. I wasn't all that concerned abou the cost, money wasn't a problem, but she surprised me. When I asked h what it would cost me, she said simply, "Whatever you would have given me, please donate to the Susan G. Komen Foundation for Breast Canc Research." Whoa! I wasn't expecting that. I asked her, "Are you sure?" Sl said, "Yes, my grandma died from breast cancer and that is a cause close my heart. It's not like I am broke or anything. This way the charity ge something, you have a wedding singer, and everyone is happy." With tha she gave me her card, I gave her mine, she gave me a hug and I asked her o last question before we left, "What brings you in here to the grocery sto with the rest of us everyday folks?" She said, "I have to eat don't I? I g tired of living like I'm not a regular person. Sometimes I have to leave th vault and come up for air." We laughed and went through the checkout lin When it was time for the big day, she came to the rehearsal right on tim sang "We Must Be In Love" by Pure Soul, "You And I" by Steve Wonder/O'Bryan, and two duets with Jonathan's brother, "Candlelight ar You", by Keith Washington and Chante Moore and "Spend My Life Wit You", by Eric Benet and Tamia. I was blown away. We decided on havir them sing "We Must be in Love" and Spend My Life with You" during th wedding. The other two songs would be reserved for the receptio Everything went as planned. Jonathan and I did not give our actual vows; w just said a basic one. Neither of us had heard what each other wrote. W wanted it that way. I even chose older flower girls and ring bearer because did not want a crying, screaming child not cooperating and throwing tantrum down the aisle during my wedding. The flower girls were Collette two 6 year old nieces (twins), and the ring bearer was Jonathan's first cousin 5 year old child. The photographer came out and took some test picture Everything was set. After the rehearsal, we all headed to a very fancy top notch restaurant in Waldorf, MD. Everyone had a good time. It wa wonderful. The bridesmaids all came to my Aunt Lena's house, where I wa staying in town. I was closer to her than my own mother. We stayed up unt late at night, watching the Color Purple on HBO and laughing about various things. The next morning, we went over to my mom's house and she had prepared an enormous breakfast. It was great, but I was too nervous to eat much. I knew I had to eat because it was going to be a long day, so I had a drop of scrambled eggs, two slices of toast with real butter and caramel coffee with French Vanilla creamer. Ok, so I ate more than I expected for the amount of nerves I had. After breakfast, Mrs. Althea came by and touched up my hairstyle. She has been my hairdresser for about 5 years. I was shocked that she gave up a Saturday, her busiest day, to be there for my wedding. That meant a lot to me. She also made sure that all of the bridesmaids and maids of honor had their hair in check. Her sister came with her and did all of our makeup. We were Hollywood ready! The photographer came by my mother's house and got some shots of all of us getting ready. Once I had on my dress, he took some shots of me in my mother's yard and in front of her big front hall mirror. I had a beautiful off white, silk Vera Wang halter dress with a 15 foot train. At 11:30am the limousine arrived and I left for the church. We took more pictures outside. The bridesmaids all piled into Camille's minivan and my mother and Aunt Lena rode with me. Uncle Philip, who I had not seen in years, rode with the photographer. It seemed like we got to the church in record time. This was my last ride in a car as a single woman. I was getting nervous. I mean, I had been married before. What if this one didn't work? The other one didn't. I was in panic. I had to take a few deep breaths. No sooner than the limo driver stopped the car and opened the door, the photographer arrived with Uncle Philip. Once again, more pictures. Camille's minivan arrived moments later and Alayna and Olivia surveyed the church to make sure the path was clear for me to enter the church. Who knows where Jonathan Daniel was, but he wasn't in the back of the church. I quickly scurried into the church and we all slid into the back into a back room. I was really getting a bad case of the nerves. I saw all of the guests (through a crack in the door) as I entered the back of the church. "Geez Louise! What am I doing?" I started to hyperventilate. There was a knock on the door. Tara Kellye was there. I told her to sing something, anything. I didn't care what she sang, just anything to change my mood. She started up with the chorus of "Hold On" by En Vogue. She remembered that was my favorite song in high school. Once she got through the chorus one good time, Alayna started the first verse, alternating with Olivia, then Camille, and then Collette and I chimed in for the next chorus. The bad nerves were lifting. Collette's husband knocked on the door and told us that Jonathan was there. It was SHOWTIME! Th processional music started. Everything was blurring together. Next thing knew, I was down the aisle halfway and Jonathan was coming into full focu through my veil. He was the most handsome man on Earth at that momen but to hear him tell it, there was no woman on Earth more beautiful than was. I almost felt like I was floating, even though my father had me tight the arm. For a minute, my feet didn't touch the floor. I was somehow o the ground, but still moving toward the altar. It's funny, even though th church was huge, it felt like I had a 10 mile walk to get to that altar, but one I got there, my heart raced, I felt a feeling of comfort and I knew that this wa the right thing to do. The pastor asked the usual, "Do you take so and s blahzay blah, blah blah." We said our "With this ring, I thee wed", our ow wedding vows, and we said the "I-do's" and we were done. WHEW. Nex it was time for the cake! The wedding reception was nothing short spectacular. Tara Kellye did her thing with the band! The music wa wonderful. We had the world's best and most buttery cake from a little cak place in Laurel, MD. Everyone had a really good time. I have to say, withou "tooting my own horn", that this was a flawless wedding. Jonathan's forme neighbor (from early childhood), who was coincidentally going to be on th cruise during Jess's wedding, caught the garter (originally he said he couldn make Jess and Wes's upcoming wedding because he was supposed to be o travel for his job – he was a there as a very casual date of one of our guest but nothing serious). Ironically, you guessed it, Camille caught the bouque Folks tried to say that Jonathan and I intentionally aimed these articles righ for them, but we know we had our backs turned and it was the fate of th universe that had them catch the items.

Our gift table was full of all kinds of presents. The photographe and his assistant were doing a marvelous job of capturing the event on film and video. I couldn't have asked for a more perfect day. This had to hav been the absolute happiest day of my entire life.

HAPPILY EVER AFTER

I got an email from Camille several months later. She sent me about 10 pictures from Wes and Jess's wedding cruise. I didn't go. I have a thing about being out on the ocean with no land in sight. I just don't enjoy myself. Anyway, she also sent me a separate picture of her and some guy. I kept trying to place where I knew him from and it just wasn't coming to me. He was really handsome. She wrote a short note with that one saying that he was Wes's friend from middle school who just happened to be on the cruise, he thought he wouldn't be able to make it, but his work travel assignment got postponed at the last minute and he was able to make the cruise. It hit me then that he was at my wedding reception and caught the garter, the former early childhood neighbor of Jonathan! Wes and the friend hadn't seen each other in a long while before my wedding reception. He seemed to have a lot of the same interests Camille had and they felt like they had known each other for a lifetime from the moment they were introduced at the wedding reception, just neither of them paid attention at the time. The universe evidently brought them back together. I'm thinking to myself, "Yeah, yeah, yeah, I have heard that one before", how this one felt like the one and blah blah blah. I kept reading and she said, "I know you are sitting there saying 'yeah, yeah, yeah, I have heard that before', but this one is different. He didn't come into the picture trying to have sex with me. He didn't run when I told him I had kids, and he doesn't seem shaken by the fact that I cann« have any more kids. He has two daughters that live with him. His wife di« in Afghanistan 5 years prior. She was serving in the Armed Forces. He w: against it, but she was already in the Armed Forces when they got marrie He owns his own company, has a close relationship with GOD, and he is li! no other man I've ever known. I think he is the one." Well what could I s: to that? Who am I to rain on her parade? After all, she could be right abo« this one. The phone rang and it was Alayna. I was glad to hear from h« She told me she got the same kind of email from Camille about the guy « the cruise. I told Alayna that maybe this one may be the one for her, the o1 that will treat her with some respect and value, unlike all the others. Alay1 giggled and said, "You know what this means?" I said, "What?" She replie "Time for us to get ready for another wedding!" With that we hung up. logged off of the computer and joined Jonathan in the sunroom. The hou: was peaceful. The twins were over Olivia's house. Rhianna was working her part-time job in Tappahannock. We were home alone. Jonathan hand« me a cup of my favorite tea, kissed me gently and I lay my head on his che as we both watched the sun set over the King and Queen County horizo Life is good! ☺☺☺☺☺

VALUABLE LESSONS SUMMARY

It is my sincere hope that you have thoroughly enjoyed this manuscript. It was based *slightly* on real experiences had by myself and my closest friends, family members, friends of family members, neighbors, and acquaintances. In writing this, it was therapeutic healing from my own personal hurts and disappointments. I found myself asking GOD why I had to endure certain things and in finishing this project I got my answers. Now I will share my new-found understanding with all of you. Some of this may be nothing new to you, for others it will give you something to think about.

Points of Enlightenment:

- *You are never so special that you can make a non-committal man commit, so don't plan according to this misconception.*
- *If a man gives the impression of being non-committal or emotionally unavailable at any point, HEED THE WARNING SIGNS! Paying attention early will save you pain and heartache later. Think about the signs!*
- *If you can only see him on certain days and you know definitely that he is not married, engaged and/or living with another woman, or otherwise occupied with a job that has him on a rotating shift (firemen, doctors, surgeons, police, etc.), then he may be juggling you with other candidates.*
- *If he doesn't acknowledge you properly on special occasions, such as your birthday, Christmas, Valentine's Day, significant milestones (1 year anniversary on up), outside of possibly being a Jehovah's Witness, he is probably not really that into you.*

- *If he carries your relationship as though he is seeing you f[right now but doesn't want to call you his actual "lady", or [though he is trying to keep the door open on the premise of "ju in case something better comes along", roll out! You don't nee to be someone's Plan B. If he is really into you and wants to g[to know you on a deeper level, not necessarily in a rush to g[engaged or married – but to keep seeing you exclusively – the[will be no need for him to keep his antennae extended to reac out for signals from other prospects. Beware of the jugglin jester; he later becomes the "Married But Looking (MBL)" man*

Don't make excuses for his behavior. If he gives excuses for n[acknowledging you at Christmas, such as "We never really discussed givin each other gifts" or he tries to make 1,000 excuses, but goes out and splurg[on his main hobby to the tune of $10,000+ cash, you know he is not seriot about how you feel or placing any real value on cultivating a lastir relationship with you. It doesn't take much to give a sister a $50 gift card [Victoria's Secret or to give you a prepackaged gift basket from Bath & Bo[Works. Even the simplest gesture shows thoughtfulness. It isn't alwa[about the size of the gift, rather the magnitude of the emphasis on yot importance that comes behind it.

You should never have to go through it alone. If the two of you are involve with armed robbery and get caught, you should not try to take the rap for hi[because you are likely to get a lesser sentence; likewise he should not ask th of you. This is just an example. My point is that if the two of you fin yourselves between a rock and a very hard place, both of you should dig yot way out of it. You cannot be the sole party responsible for the actions [everyone else on earth. His lack of support shows what you really mean t him: **NOT MUCH**.

YOU SHOULD NOT BE BY YOURSELF IN THE MIDST OF A RELATIONSHIP!

If you find yourself going to couples' events alone or he is overly reluctant to go with you to events, this is a red flag. Outside of work commitments that cannot be changed or some medical situation, there is no harm in him attending a cookout, family picnic, Off-Broadway plays, or concerts with you and vice versa. If you are doing all of the coordinating of attendance for events and gatherings, take a minute and examine that. Why is he afraid to be out with you? I bet he isn't afraid to be "in" with you nor is he uncomfortable with you naked between the sheets. The same comfort and willingness to hop into the bed should be exhibited in just spending time with you. If you find yourself spending more of your time with him behind closed doors than anywhere else, what does that say about how he views you?

You do not have to do all of the calling and pursuing. If this man has a bona fide interest in you, when he hasn't heard from you within a reasonable amount of time, he will call you.

GET TO KNOW THE OTHER PERSON WELL BEFORE YOU GET INTIMATE

Make him prove to you why he should be allowed to "taste your cookies". After all, you shouldn't be "giving samples" to just anyone.

If a guy is too eager to get close to you in the very beginning of the game, get out your cattle prod. If he is anxious to kiss you on a first date and tries to feel you up or keeps throwing heavy sexual innuendos your way, pull your parking brake! Don't feed into the advances in the early stages of the game. 9 times out of 10 there is a possibility that he is only out to "get it" from you in the first place. Once he gets it, the precedent has been set and he won't feel compelled to wine you and dine you, just to get your clothes off every chance he can. This cheats YOU out of crucial bonding and getting to know each other. Intimacy in the first inning of the game pushes the game itself into fast forward. Think of the situation as though it is an old fashioned VHS tape. If you go right to the intimacy within the early, delicate stage of the relationship, it is the same as pushing the forward button and stopping at the last 10 minutes of the movie. You have missed all of the storyline, punch lines, details, etc. The same applies in courting.

FINAL THOUGHTS - I'M JUST GOING TO LEAVE IT RIGHT HERE:

If he is inconsistent with calling you and showing regular interest, don't dr(those draws. Don't get taken by him when he does call. Know how differentiate sincere interest from someone pursuing just sexual pleasure. L your homework!!! Find out the guy's background. Yes, do an internet sear(or any other kind of investigative search available. It is important to find o(early in the game if he is an ax murderer or escaped psycho. Don't be afra(to take the time necessary to get to know him. Ask questions!!! It's for yo(safety!!! *****

LOOK FOR THESE EXCITING TITLES, COMING SOON:

BLOOD WAS EVERYWHERE ©   **-Releasing in 2015-**

Synopsis

Imagine your car being totaled and the ghost of the other driver follows you indefinitely, serving as a quasi guardian angel while the ghost of his murdered brother torments your best friend. In this riveting tale of 3 best friends from different walks of life, that is exactly what happens. Galileo Hunter is a beautiful, sophisticated, metropolitan woman with a thriving career when her world goes topsy-turvy after a young man is shot and totals her parked car as he attempts to drive himself to the local hospital. During a trip back to her hometown for business, the driver's brother randomly assaults her in her hotel room and ends up dying from defense wounds delivered with the aid of Galileo's best friend, Avery Collishaw. To add insult to injury, the other best friend, Madison Gardner, seems to have a near perfect life with her successful businessman of a husband, 2 doting children, and a new baby on the way. Is it real or just a façade?   As Madison's seemingly perfect marriage takes unexpected turns and twists, she must try to maintain appearances, salvage her sanity, and join forces with Galileo and Avery to help both lost spirits cross over into eternity.

DUAL MISTRESS ©   **-Releasing in 2015-**

Synopsis

Gemilla Merrick has it all together, except when it comes to her choices in men. Torn between a passionate, Earth moving sexual affair with a fickle man who is stuck in complacency, and being wined and dined by a debonair, sophisticated anchorman on the nightly news, she has to decide what is important, what is intolerable, and face the fact that if she could take the best qualities out of both men and roll them into one, she would be set. Unfortunately, she discovers that life isn't that simple!

20470049R00065

Made in the USA
Middletown, DE
27 May 2015